### "Maybe I could help you out with your boys, too," he said.

"I'm not sure that would work," Delia replied. "They'll just see you as a threat." An image sprang into her mind of a scarecrow—stuffed with straw, incapable of feeling any pain. "The most helpful thing would be to have a scarecrow to let them work out their worst behavior so they can get over it!"

"A human scarecrow?" Elias said, his eyebrows rising.

"I was joking! I can't ask you to put up with their bad attitudes."

"It's not a bad idea, actually." Elias plucked a muffin off the plate and peeled back the paper. "Your sons want to protect you and take care of you like their *daet* did. They need to talk about all that—work it out. If you helped me to sort out my daughter's anger, I could take a couple of weeks of teenage angst for you."

Elias cast her a heart-stopping lopsided smile. Was he offering what she thought he was offering? And dare she consider it?

T0112718

**Patricia Johns** is a *Publishers Weekly* bestselling author who writes from Alberta, Canada, where she lives with her husband and son. She writes Amish romances that will leave you yearning for a simpler life. You can find her at patriciajohns.com and on social media, where she loves to connect with her readers. Drop by her website and you might find your next read!

Visit the Author Profile page at LoveInspired.com for more titles.

# Her Pretend Amish Beau

PATRICIA JOHNS

## LOVE INSPIRED
INSPIRATIONAL ROMANCE

If you purchased this book without a cover you should be aware that this book is stolen property. It was reported as "unsold and destroyed" to the publisher, and neither the author nor the publisher has received any payment for this "stripped book."

## LOVE INSPIRED®
### INSPIRATIONAL ROMANCE

Recycling programs for this product may not exist in your area.

ISBN-13: 978-1-335-93664-6

Her Pretend Amish Beau

Copyright © 2024 by Patricia Johns

All rights reserved. No part of this book may be used or reproduced in any manner whatsoever without written permission.

Without limiting the author's and publisher's exclusive rights, any unauthorized use of this publication to train generative artificial intelligence (AI) technologies is expressly prohibited.

This is a work of fiction. Names, characters, places and incidents are either the product of the author's imagination or are used fictitiously. Any resemblance to actual persons, living or dead, businesses, companies, events or locales is entirely coincidental.

For questions and comments about the quality of this book, please contact us at CustomerService@Harlequin.com.

® is a trademark of Harlequin Enterprises ULC.

Love Inspired
22 Adelaide St. West, 41st Floor
Toronto, Ontario M5H 4E3, Canada
www.LoveInspired.com

**Printed in Lithuania**

MIX
Paper | Supporting responsible forestry
FSC® C021394

There is a friend that sticketh closer than a brother.
—*Proverbs* 18:24

To my husband and son. Life just keeps getting sweeter, so long as we are together. I love you!

# *Chapter One*

Delia Swarey stood in her messy kitchen. Dirty dishes were stacked on the crumb-scattered counters, and the floor hadn't been swept since yesterday. They were in a busy time here at the Swarey Flower Farm, and in order for her and her four boys to get the outdoor work done, something had to slide. That turned out to be her housework.

Delia ran her hands down her gray work apron. It neatly covered a pink cape dress. Even without anyone to see her inside the house, she did better with her own appearance than she did her countertops. Her dark brown hair, highlighted with a few gray strands, was pulled into a bun at the nape of her neck and covered with a crisp, white *kapp*.

A knock drew her away from the mess, and she headed over to the side door and pulled it open with a tired sigh. A teenage girl stood on the step. She wore a pink cape dress in a darker hue than Delia's, and her blond hair was pinned back neatly underneath a white *kapp*.

"Hello, I'm Violet Lehman." The slim girl had her head cocked to one side, and one hand planted on her hip. "I'm Judith and Bernard Lehman's granddaughter from next door, and I was wondering if you might have a job for me to do."

"Are you here visiting?" Delia asked.

"*Yah*, my *daet* and I came to help my grandparents move to my aunt Dina's house."

"Right…" She'd been so busy that she hadn't been keeping up with her neighbors' lives, and she felt bad about that. Violet's father was Elias Lehman—she knew him from grade school. "I didn't realize you'd arrived yet. I thought—"

"It's okay," Violet said, and she glanced over her shoulder furtively. "The thing is, I'm here for a couple of weeks, and I want a job, if you'll give me one."

"A job?"

"*Yah*. I can do most things. I'll weed and hoe, water plants, carry buckets—whatever you need. If you'll pay me."

Delia glanced back at the messy kitchen. Would the girl want to clean up?

"How do you feel about housework?" Delia asked.

"I was hoping—" Violet's face fell "—I was hoping for real work."

As if cooking and cleaning wasn't real work! Any woman who had to keep up with it all knew just how much work it really was. It was women's work, but she thought she understood.

"How old are you?" she asked.

"Thirteen."

Delia might have guessed older, but at this age, it could be hard to tell. Violet was nearing the age of graduating from the eighth grade and would be getting a job after that, anyway.

"And how does your *daet* feel about you asking me for work?" Delia raised her eyebrows.

Violet's cheeks pinked. "He...doesn't know."

"I can't very well give you work without your *daet*'s permission," Delia said. "I'm sorry, Violet. As much as I could use some extra help around here right now..."

"You could let me start now, and I'll ask him at dinnertime," Violet said quickly. "He won't mind, especially if he knows I already started. Then he'll see that it's just fine."

Delia wasn't about to be part of a girl manipulating her father, and she spotted a tall, lean man over by the fence. He pushed his hat back on his head. He had a full, dark married beard and his sleeves were rolled up to reveal tanned forearms. Was that Elias? He had broad shoulders and an easy way of standing that was familiar. She hadn't seen him since his wedding twenty years ago, when he hadn't grown his beard yet. He was three years older than she was, and Delia had just turned forty-one this year.

"Is that your *daet*?" Delia nodded over Violet's shoulder.

The girl turned and her shoulders slumped ever so little. *"Yah."*

"Well, let's bring him over and sort this out," Delia said. "I could use the help, and I'll pay you for it, but I need his permission."

Delia waved, and Elias leaned down and slid between the rails of the fence, then headed over in their direction with an easy swagger, and Delia repressed the urge to check her *kapp* with her fingertips. He'd certainly matured into a nice-looking man, she had to admit.

"Delia!" Elias smiled as he ambled up. "I see you've met my daughter."

"*Yah*, Violet and I just met." Delia smiled at the girl. "She's a lovely young woman."

"*Danke*, I couldn't agree more," Elias said, then he sobered. "I heard about Zeke. I'm sorry, Delia."

"*Danke*, but you understand that pain. I heard about Wanda," she replied. They'd both lost their spouses in the last few years.

"*Yah*, it's been…hard." Elias looked down at his daughter, then sighed. "The Lord gave, and the Lord has taken away."

"Blessed be the name of the Lord," Delia murmured, completing the Scripture reference. "It's not always so easy to accept it, though, is it?"

"Not at all," he agreed. "I'm sorry to bring up sad topics. My daughter and I are here in Redemption helping my parents move to my sister Dina's place. They just built a new *dawdie hus*, and my parents will be much more comfortable over there. My other sister Mary and her husband are taking over this house, so there's a lot to prepare."

"She mentioned that," Delia replied. "I was talking with your mother about it not so long ago, and I thought there was another month still. But we've been so busy here with flower orders for some big chain stores that I think the time got away from me. Without Zeke, it falls to me and the boys to keep it all running, and I'll admit it hasn't been easy."

Violet sent Delia a hopeful look that made the girl suddenly look younger, and Delia's heart melted. With four boys of her own, she had a soft place in her heart for little girls. She'd hoped to enlarge her family with a daughter before Zeke died, but it hadn't been Gott's will.

"Elias, Violet mentioned she might have some free time to help me out around here," Delia said, casting the girl a smile. "I don't know if you'd be okay with it, but if she'd be willing to help me and the boys with some garden work, I'd pay her for her time."

Violet's smile was a grateful one. What could Delia say? She'd enjoy having a girl around here, too. Being the *mamm* of four boys left her perpetually outnumbered, and while Violet wouldn't exactly even things out, it would be nice, all the same.

As if on cue, Delia's two middle boys, Thomas and Aaron, came out of a greenhouse and headed in their direction. Their gloves were dirty, and they wore rubber boots. They'd been watering the more delicate rose bushes. She smiled indulgently in their direction.

"Meet two of my boys," Delia said. "This is Thomas—he's fifteen—and Aaron, who's fourteen." The boys arrived at the house then. "Boys, meet Violet Lehman. She's the daughter of my friend, Elias."

Thomas and Aaron exchanged a look, not to be distracted by a girl, apparently, because they then eyed Elias suspiciously.

"Is this a friend like the man from Bird in Hand?" Aaron asked, lowering his voice, but still loud enough to be heard by Elias, and Delia felt her face heat.

"No, Aaron. Not like that. This is Judith and Bernard's son and granddaughter."

"Oh, good," Thomas said, shaking his head. "Sorry. There have been some men interested in courting our *mamm*. Just making sure you weren't one of them."

"Thomas!" Delia gave him an annoyed look. "I don't have a lineup of men asking for my hand. You make one or two callers sound like a flock!"

"There were three of them," Aaron countered.

"Over a span of two years," Delia replied, and she looked over at Elias to find an amused smile tickling his lips.

"Daet, can I work for Delia?" Violet asked earnestly.

Delia was glad for the distraction from this current direction the conversation had taken.

"Working with boys?" Elias said, and he looked about ready to shake his head in the negative.

"I'll have to work with boys when I get a real job, Daet," Violet said, and she darted a cautious look in Delia's sons' direction. "And these ones seem decent enough. Their *mamm* looks like she'd keep them in line."

Aaron's freckled face blushed red then, and Thomas barked out a laugh. "Our *mamm* is downright terrifying."

"I am not!" Delia said, shaking a finger at them. "You two, get back to work! We've got lots to do."

Thomas shot her a grin that never ceased to soften her up, and Aaron eyed Violet once more as if he didn't quite know what to make of her. But they did as they were told and headed back in the direction of the greenhouses.

Delia let her gaze move over the rows of greenhouses to the flower plots beyond—row upon row of lavender, daisies, chrysanthemums and baby's breath had come into bloom. The color and the scent drew tourists in from the side of the road, and they'd take pictures.

"What kind of work do you need her to do?" Elias asked.

"She'd have to take direction from the boys," Delia

said. "They're watering plants and adding fertilizer. Soon enough we'll be picking stems for a large flower order. It's careful work—we can't be damaging the blooms— but I'm sure she can do it."

Violet shot her a relieved smile. She'd probably thought that Delia was going to offer her housework. Well, Delia wouldn't mind an opportunity to tidy up her own kitchen for a change from the outdoor work.

"Well…" Elias sighed. "Okay, if you're offering her the work."

"Aaron! Thomas!" Delia called. The boys turned. "Take Violet with you and show her what she can do to help out, would you? You can get her a pair of my rubber boots and one of my aprons!"

*"Danke!"* Violet said with a brilliant smile, and she jogged off in the boys' direction.

"You don't have to worry about my sons," Delia said. "They are well-raised boys, I can assure you. My oldest, Ezekiel, already has a girlfriend of his own. And my youngest is only eleven. You've seen the biggest danger just now."

Elias nodded. "I have a feeling your boys would be good *kinner.*" He looked in the direction of his daughter's receding form as she ambled next to the boys toward the largest greenhouse. The aprons and boots were kept there. "Did she come asking for work?"

*"Yah,* she did," Delia replied. "I guess she's eager to make her own money."

Elias nodded slowly, then stopped nodding and shook his head. "She's had a hard time since her *mamm* passed. She's got her own way of seeing things."

"How has she been dealing with it all?" Delia asked.

"She's gotten rebellious."

"I'm sorry."

"Me, too. I only want to keep her safe."

"But if her biggest rebellion is getting a job—" Delia shrugged.

"It's not." He winced, and for a moment, he seemed to hold his breath. Then he exhaled in a rush. "Delia, I know it's been ages since we've been friends, but can I count on your discretion?"

"Of course."

"She's been idealizing the Englisher ways. She's got a little radio that she listens to their music on, and I caught her with a tube of lipstick a month ago. Lipstick!"

"Well, she can't get away with wearing it," Delia said. The Amish didn't wear makeup, and lipstick would stand out, no matter how subtle the color.

"Not here, but if she were in town…" He sighed.

"I know, I know," she said. "You worry that she's going to attract the wrong attention."

"Exactly. And that she's flouting rules for the sake of being rebellious. If she's doing that now at the age of thirteen, what will she be doing at seventeen when it's time for her *Rumspringa* and she gets a bit more freedom?"

"I understand that worry," she said. "I used to worry about Ezekiel, but he's in his *Rumspringa* now, and the worst thing he's done is play music on a radio in his buggy. Oh…and he bought a pair of Englisher running shoes, but he hardly wears them."

"It's more than that. It's the loss of her *mamm*. I know it was particularly hard on her, and she's angry, but she doesn't have anyone to blame."

"No one but Gott," she murmured.

Delia understood that anger. She'd felt it for a little while after her husband died. Why hadn't Gott intervened? Why had he chosen to take her husband right when she'd needed him most? She'd worked through it, but then she was a grown woman. How could a girl know how to make sense of such a loss? That kind of emotional turmoil wasn't Violet's fault.

"How have your boys dealt with Zeke's passing?" Elias asked.

They were getting right to the personal business, weren't they? But she could see the worry in Elias's eyes. Not many people could understand their situation, she knew. Losing a spouse, and then carrying on raising children as a single parent, was the hardest thing a person could do.

"You saw how protective they are of me," Delia replied. "They're like roosters around here, and I'm the only hen to protect. They hate it when I even entertain the idea of another man in my life. I've tried talking to them about it, but they don't want a new *daet*. And they figure they can take care of me themselves. They think I'll forget about a new husband if they can carry the burden on those boyish shoulders. I don't want them to do that. It's sweet, but…"

"Wrong," he finished for her.

Delia leaned against the doorframe. "*Yah*. Wrong. But will they listen?"

"Have they been questioning their faith?" he asked, lowering his voice.

"No…not that I know of," Delia said. "Do you really think Violet will leave the faith?"

He spread his hands. "How can I know? She's told

me a couple of times already that she wants to go English when it comes time for her *Rumspringa*. She wants a job so she can save up her money. She'll change her mind on that, won't she?"

She knew what Elias wanted her to say—that Violet would forget about it, outgrow the ideas, and everything would turn out perfectly given a bit of time. But how could Delia know that? He wanted reassurance that Delia couldn't provide. She shook her head, and instead said, "They keep us hopping."

"Do they ever."

How long had it been since Delia had had an honest conversation like this with another parent? She'd talked to other mothers, but these days she found herself reassuring everyone that she was doing just fine. She didn't know why she'd fallen into that habit. Her sisters and brothers had all left for other communities, so she didn't have the support. For the most part, Delia was fine. But telling other married women that she wanted to get married again felt almost like she was envying them their healthy, happy marriages. And maybe she was! But she didn't like to admit it. Talking with Elias felt different, though. He had his own struggles, and he was in the same situation she was.

Delia met Elias's gaze and she smiled. "It's good to see you again, Elias."

It was comforting, somehow, to see an old friend who could sympathize.

"It's good to see you, too," he said.

"Did you want to come inside?" she asked, and she glanced over her shoulder at the messy kitchen and winced. "Actually, my kitchen is a mess. I'm going to be honest with you—I can't keep up with proper house-work and with the farm work. So when I have to choose between a job that will keep money coming in and one that will just give me a clean counter again, I choose the income."

"Understandable." He met her gaze easily. "And if you're offering to let me come in, I won't judge."

Delia stood back and gestured through the door. "Then come on in, Elias. You'll see the worst of my kitchen, but I suppose it'll make us truly friends if you don't faint."

Elias laughed at her joke and came inside. She watched him as he glanced around the kitchen—the unfinished dishes, the cluttered counter, the messy table. He didn't look alarmed, and she headed over to clear off the table and give it a wipe. There were still a few dishes from the boys' snacks on the table, and bread crusts from un-finished midmorning sandwiches.

"I don't know why I just told you all that about Vio-let," Elias said. "You're easy to talk to."

"I'm also in the same wagon, so to speak," she said. "It's not easy parenting alone."

"I've been working hard at keeping my mouth shut in Indiana, hoping Violet will settle down and I'll fig-ure out how to help her adjust. I don't want her reputa-tion to be damaged. Her struggles should be private."

"I try to keep up appearances, too," Delia replied, carrying a stack of dishes to the counter and returning with a wet cloth. "I hate being 'Poor Delia.' I don't want to feel sorry for myself, and I don't want other people feeling sorry for me, either."

"That's pride," Elias said with a rueful smile. "I

should know. I'm the same way. Not that it's working very well, but I try."

Delia wiped off the table, took a pair of boys' boots off the seat of one chair and carried them to the mudroom where they belonged.

"You know, I could talk to Violet," Delia said as she returned. "If she's working over here, I might have an opportunity. *Kinner* can be like that—they won't hear a word from the parent who loves them more than life, but they'll consider something from a stranger. Maybe I can give her a word of wisdom."

"You'd do that?" Elias asked.

"Elias, of course! We're all in this together, and parenting is hard."

"Maybe I could help you out with your boys, too," he said.

Her boys would only close the circle and think that Elias wanted more from her. They'd get defensive and very likely rude. She couldn't have that.

"I'm not sure that would work," Delia replied. "They'll just see you as a threat." An image sprang into her mind of a scarecrow—stuffed with straw and incapable of feeling any pain whatsoever. "The most helpful thing would be to have a scarecrow to let them work out their worst behavior so they can get over it and put it behind them!" She smiled ruefully and deposited a plate of muffins into the center of the table, within reach of her guest. "But don't worry, I'll figure something out."

"A human scarecrow?" Elias said, his eyebrows rising.

"I was joking! I can't ask you to put up with their bad

attitudes. They can be a handful. I love them dearly, but I also know my boys."

"It's not a bad idea, actually." Elias plucked a muffin off the plate and peeled back the paper. "Your sons want to protect you and take care of you like their *daet* did. It's part of being male—that drive to protect a woman. And they need to talk about all that—work it out. Sometimes it's hard to show our weakness in front of extended family and the ones who know us best. But you and I might be able to help each other. If you helped me to sort out my daughter's anger, I could take a couple of weeks of teenage angst for you."

And Elias cast her a heart-stopping lopsided smile. Her heart skipped a beat. Was he offering what she thought he was offering? And dare she consider it?

Elias wasn't even sure why he'd offered it! Standing in to let four teenage boys take out their confused feelings on him? But she was offering to talk to his own confused teen, and he was grateful—maybe too grateful. And Delia was comfortingly beautiful. She had creamy skin with natural color in her cheeks, and eyes that made him want to smile for no reason whatsoever. Her dark hair had a few strands of silver now. When he knew her years ago, she'd been sandy blonde, but time had darkened her hair and softened her figure.

That shouldn't matter. It didn't really, he told himself firmly. It wasn't like he was ready to take on a whole new family, either!

The side door banged open and a young boy came inside.

"Mamm, I need a Band-Aid!" he hollered and stopped short when he saw Elias. "Oh. Sorry."

"Where did you hurt yourself?" Delia asked. "And this is Elias, an old friend of mine. Elias, this is my youngest, Moses. He's eleven. He's my almost-teen, but I lump him in with the others."

Elias gave him a nod, and Moses's gaze turned shrewd. He was a skinny kid with a spattering of freckles across his nose. The sun had left him pink. He was suspecting more than a friendly visit, it would seem.

"Show me where you're hurt," Delia said.

Moses pulled up a pant leg, and there was a smear of blood on one shin. Delia tutted, got a cloth and opened a tin of Band-Aids.

"How did you do that?" she asked.

"On the fence."

"You boys leave more of your own flesh on that fence," she said. "You could walk around to the gate, you know."

"It's too far. I like going over."

Elias couldn't help but smile at that. In his home, it was all about school drama, deep sighs and his daughter telling him he couldn't possibly understand anything about the right running shoes to go with her dresses. But he remembered being a boy who climbed over fences and skinned his knees. Boy problems were refreshing.

Delia bandaged Moses up and then looked out the side window.

"Did you finish weeding the fourth row?" she asked.

"*Yah*, that's why I was going over the fence. I was going to get an apple from the tree."

"Those are green," she said. "You'll get a stomach-ache."

"Can I have a muffin, then?"

"Sure." Delia handed him one and pointed him toward the door. "If you want a break, that's okay, but after that you can either help me with dishes or check for eggs in the henhouse."

"Aw..." Moses made a big show of sighing. Delia was unmoved. "Okay. I'll check for eggs."

"Good choice!" Delia shot her son a smile. "And thank you for your hard work, Moses. You're really growing up."

The boy's shoulders straightened at the compliment, and he headed for the door. When the screen door flapped shut behind him, Delia took the Band-Aids back to the cupboard. She was strong and competent, and there was wisdom in those dark eyes of hers. He felt better just being in her kitchen.

"And I haven't even offered you something to drink!" Delia said suddenly. "What kind of a hostess am I?"

"Don't worry about it," Elias said. "Sit down."

Delia blushed a little and pulled out a chair. She reached for a muffin.

"The thing is," Elias said, "you're the only one I've talked to in two years who really gets it. The Early Widowed Club is a lonely group. There aren't too many of us, and no one else really understands the challenges, even though they try. And your boys look like good *kinner* to me. I think I could probably get them to talk, especially if they thought I was trying to court you. They'd have a whole lot to say about that."

That was how boys worked—they'd open up if they figured it was for a cause. Otherwise, they'd be tight-lipped.

"You might be too brave," she replied with a low laugh.

"What happened to the other three men who tried courting you?" Elias asked.

"My boys chased them off," she replied. "Or I caved in and called it off because my boys couldn't handle it. It amounts to the same thing."

It did. Her boys were locking things down around here—no matter how good their intentions were about taking care of their mother. And his daughter was going wild on him and threatening to leave the Amish faith just as soon as she could run away. That thought chilled his blood. But Elias might have a solution...

"If our *kinner* thought that we were courting," Elias said slowly, "it might give us time to help them get over a few things."

Delia turned her head to the side, then looked back at him.

"How would Violet feel about you courting someone?" Delia asked.

Through the window, Elias could just see the front of the biggest greenhouse. The door opened and his daughter came out clad in a dark apron and gum boots. One of the boys gestured out toward a garden plot and she turned after them and disappeared from sight.

"It might do Violet good to see that her Amish life can go on," Elias said quietly. "I think that might be part of her problem. Her *mamm* is dead, and she can't imagine life just...going on without her, you know? She'd rather leave everything behind than face life without her *mamm* in it. And I understand. I just can't seem to make it better for her. But if she could see that life can go on with her mother's memory intact, I think it would help her."

"You do understand her," Delia said quietly.

"She doesn't think I do."

Delia nodded. "*Yah.* It's hard for all of us—harder for the *kinner*, for sure."

The more he thought on it, the more this idea seemed to be a good one. Add to that, his parents had already been hinting strongly that he should be looking in Delia's direction for a new wife, even though he'd told them that he wasn't ready for anything like that.

"My boys aren't ready for me to date, but this might actually help," Delia went on. "I can't let them keep guarding me like they're doing. This might be just the thing to change the tone around here. If they could face the thought of me spending time with a man, we can sort out all those confusing feelings—without my sons being an actual threat to a new relationship."

"And if I don't get Violet talking about her feelings, I might lose her for good when she's old enough to make a choice for the faith," he agreed. "This might get her talking. I think it's worth a shot."

He looked down at Delia, and he could see the emotions flickering across her face, until they finally settled into a smile.

"So…for the *kinner*?" she asked.

"*Yah.*"

"How would we do this? I don't want to lie to them," she said.

That was a problem. He didn't want to lie, either, but sometimes parents kept some information back from *kinner*, for their own good.

"We could simply tell them that we're old friends, and we like each other..." Elias paused. "I know it's been a while, but I always did like you. So that wouldn't be a lie."

She dropped her gaze. "I thought you were nice, too."

"And we could tell them that we want to spend more time together and see where things go," he suggested.

"Technically all true," she agreed with a nod. "Except we're seeing where things go with our *kinner* instead of each other."

"*Yah*, exactly." It was a deft side step.

"And when it's time for you to go back to Indiana?" she asked.

"We tell them that we enjoyed getting to know each other and that we'll stay good friends, but that we decided to keep things on a friendship level."

Delia nodded slowly, and her lips pursed in thought for a moment. Then she nodded again.

"It wouldn't be bad for them to see how that works," she agreed. "How many young people cause untold grief because they don't know how to simply let go and move on when a romance doesn't work out? But if they can see two mature people spending time together in a virtuous way and moving on without hard feelings, it might be a valuable lesson for the future for all of them. That's a skill, you know."

"*Yah*, I know it." This might be even better than he thought. He might not have a wife to help him in the raising of his daughter anymore, but a good friend might make up the difference. "So...are you willing?"

"I am." Another, even brighter smile broke over her face.

And he felt a flood of relief. This might be a reckless idea in some ways, but sometimes Gott provided just the solution when a man needed it. And Delia seemed like the perfect solution to him.

## Chapter Two

Delia wrote down the three hours of work that Violet had put in that day in a little notebook. Violet's help with the weeding had meant Delia had time to clean the kitchen from top to bottom, and she'd swept and mopped the rest of the house. Everything smelled so much cleaner inside, and she'd whipped up a dinner of beef and barley soup, sandwiches, and some leftover chicken from the night before.

"It's so clean in here," Moses said as he came tramping inside. At eleven, he was no longer "the baby" of the family, and he worked just as hard as his older brothers did all summer long until school would start again at the end of September.

"And I want it to stay this way," Delia replied. "I want you to sweep out the mudroom after dinner, Moses. And make sure all the boots are neatly on mats."

Moses knew better than to complain, but he did sigh as he came into the kitchen. The other boys weren't far behind him. Aaron came backing up out of the mudroom to make room for his brothers, the soles of his rubber boots full of dirt.

"Uh-uh. Aaron—if one foot comes out of the mudroom…" Delia said, raising her voice.

Delia didn't really have an end to that threat. What would she do? Probably just throw her hands up and give up entirely. But boys didn't care about that. Aaron, though, at fourteen, was a handsome young man who knew the power of his charms, and he shot his mother a grin and shouldered back into the small mudroom with Thomas and Ezekiel Jr. Ezekiel was the eldest at seventeen. He was as tall as his *daet* had been at a little less than six feet, and while he was very close to being a man, he wasn't quite there yet. She could still see the boy in him.

As the boys elbowed around and got their hands washed in the mudroom, Delia got the meal onto the table—the sandwich fixings piled high onto plates so that the boys could make their own. They knew what they liked, and they'd eat their sandwiches with the meat nearly an inch thick when they were really hungry. There was one rule at her table—if you take it, you eat it. Period. After that, it was a free-for-all.

Ezekiel and Aaron came out of the mudroom and to the table. Chairs scraped as they got into their usual seats.

"So how did Violet do today?" Delia asked as Thomas joined the rest of his brothers at the table. Thomas was only fifteen, but he was a couple of inches taller than Ezekiel already, although he hadn't filled out yet.

"She worked hard," Thomas said. "Ezekiel sent her back to redo some weeding she'd missed, and she did it."

That was good that she could accept correction. If she couldn't, they wouldn't be able to use her on the farm. These next couple of weeks with the big flower shipments were too important.

"I mean, Violet rolled her eyes first, but she did go back and redo it," Ezekiel said.

"Are all girls like that?" Aaron asked.

"Like what?" Delia asked.

"Full of attitude," Aaron replied.

*"Yah,"* Ezekiel said with a laugh. "But in Violet's defense, I don't think she's ever worked a job before."

"So you like her well enough?" Delia asked. "You'll be okay working with her for a couple of weeks?"

"Hey, someone to help get the work done is fine by me," Thomas said. "I'm not sure I like that she's getting paid and we aren't, though."

"She's getting paid?" Moses protested. "That's not fair!"

"It's not that much," Ezekiel said, and he reached for the bread and the butter to start his sandwich. "Besides, I just got my own buggy, and Thomas and Aaron are getting their own calves to raise for market, and you're getting a scooter to replace your old one. So it's all going to balance out. We might not get paid in dollars, but we do have things coming."

"A full-grown steer for market can make a good amount," Aaron agreed. "I'm going to make a decent profit off that calf when it's grown."

Thomas remained silent, and Ezekiel dished up a bowl of soup and passed it to Delia. She accepted it with a smile. Ezekiel was thoughtful that way—always making sure she had food in front of her. Then he started dishing up his brothers' bowls, too.

"This is your farm, boys," Delia said. "This is your roof over your head. One day the four of you will inherit this farm, too. And sometimes we hire help."

"This is the first time I know of," Thomas said.

"When you were all very small, your *daet* hired help," she replied. "You don't remember it because you were a toddler, but there are times when a farmer needs some extra man power around the place. And Violet needed something to occupy her time, and I finally got to clean up this kitchen properly. I think we're ahead."

The boys grudgingly agreed and dug into the sandwich fixings. When they'd all gotten their soup, Delia had them bow their heads for prayer. After a moment of silence, their heads popped back up and they dove into the food.

"So what do you think of Elias?" Delia asked and sipped a spoonful of soup. The beef and barley soup had turned out rather well, if she did say so herself. This was what happened when she actually had time at the stove instead of rushing around all the time.

"Are you hiring Elias, too?" Ezekiel asked past a mouthful of sandwich.

"Hiring him?" That hadn't occurred to her at all. "No, he's only in Redemption because he's helping his parents move to his sister's place. He's well and truly busy enough. I was asking because—"

How was she supposed to say this? Carefully. That was how.

"Who is he, exactly?" Thomas asked with a frown. "I don't think we've ever met him before."

"No, you haven't met him. He's from long before any of you were born. He's an old friend from grade school. He moved to another community and got married there and had Violet. His wife passed away about a year and a half ago, and we have that in common." Delia reached for the bread, meat and mayonnaise.

"So, he's interested in courting you," Aaron concluded.

"He is?" Moses interjected. "Violet's *daet* wants to court our *mamm*?"

"We'll be spending some time together," Delia said.

"He's courting her," Thomas said, his jaw tightening.

There it was—the fight they always put up at the thought of any man showing her romantic interest.

"And what if he were?" Delia asked. "What if Elias were courting me? What if he cared about me and wanted to think about a future together? Would that be so terrible?"

Her sons looked at her, varying degrees of disapproval on all their faces. It wouldn't matter who the man was, she'd get this response from the boys.

"What would be so wrong with a man getting to know me?" she went on. "Am I not a nice woman? Don't I cook moderately well? Am I so old-looking now?"

"No, Mamm, you're wonderful," Aaron said earnestly.

"*Yah*, you're beautiful!" Moses said. "And you're a great cook!"

"It isn't *you* that's the problem," Thomas said, then took a big bite of sandwich and had to talk past the food in his mouth. "It's him."

"I don't like him," Ezekiel said.

"Me, neither," Aaron said.

"You don't know him!" Delia interjected.

"We've seen his type, Mamm," Aaron said. "The men who see a widow with a big, profitable farm, and they figure they'd like to take that off your hands and let you spend the rest of your days in the kitchen."

As if getting to spend time in her own home, cleaning it up and keeping it that way, cooking for her family, and getting to sit down and relax with some needlework was such a punishment! How many nights had she lain in bed remembering the days when she could do just that, when Zeke would come inside and give her a kiss and tell her that her cooking was the best in Pennsylvania?

"I wouldn't mind that so much," Delia said. "My kitchen is normally a disaster."

"It's *our* farm," Ezekiel said. "You and Daet built it up together. And we've been working it as long as we can remember. We don't need some man to trot in here thinking he knows flower farming better than we do."

This was an old argument. They'd brought up these very worries with the last man to show her interest. Mind, they'd had a right to worry that last time, since he'd had an inheritance coming that required he be married.

"No one is taking the farm from us!" Delia said. "But if a man did want to get to know me—"

"Then we'd have to decide what we think of him, right?" Moses interrupted. "That's the deal, isn't it? You won't marry some man and make him our new *daet* if we don't like him, right?"

"We already don't like him," Thomas said.

"What don't you like about him?" Delia asked. "You haven't even met him."

"He sent his daughter over first, didn't he?" Thomas said. "He wasn't even brave enough to do it on his own."

"No, Violet came over on her own," Delia said. "Her father didn't want her working, and I kind of stood up for her there. She wants to work, and I think that some work is good for a girl."

"I'm sure there's enough work over with her grand-parents," Ezekiel said.

"I thought you all liked her."

"We do. We're just trying to figure out what's going on here," her eldest son replied. "Mamm… Is Elias courting you?"

"Elias is going to spend some time with me," Delia said firmly. And that was the honest truth. "That's what he's doing. And I like him. I hope that the four of you will be polite to him and find something you like about him, because in the past you've been very negative about any man who might have shown me some interest. And that isn't fair."

"What's his financial situation like?" Ezekiel asked.

"That's not your business!" Delia replied. "You can-not go around asking grown men about their money. I've raised you better than that."

"It certainly is our business if he wants to court our *mamm*," Thomas said. "If he's broke and looking for a farm to sell—"

"Boys, that's quite enough!" Delia said. "You just make up the worst-case scenarios in your minds and decide it's the truth. You don't know Elias!"

"Do you know him?" Aaron asked, and suddenly he looked a whole lot older than his fourteen years.

She sighed. They were always like this, and she ei-ther had to take these boys in hand, or she'd be a very well-protected widow for the rest of her days.

"I used to know him," she said. "And we're both par-ents raising our *kinner* after a death, and we understand each other—we know what that is like." Suddenly her chin trembled, and she felt tears welling up inside her. She hated when she got weepy like this at the thought of their loss. "It's harder than you boys think."

"Oh, Mamm…" Ezekiel sighed. "We don't mean to make you feel bad. Maybe we can do more around here, right, guys? We can do more?"

"*Yah*, we'll do more," the boys echoed their elder brother.

"And we'll keep the kitchen cleaner, too," Moses said. "I'll sweep out the mudroom when we're done eating, like you asked."

"And we'll do the dishes, too," Aaron said. "Without you telling us."

"She's been doing men's work, you know." Thomas turned to his brothers. "And it's no doubt she's tired. We men will take care of it. Mamm should be inside and getting more rest. There's four of us. We can make that happen."

It was sweet of him, but he was wrong about one thing. They were boys, not men.

"You absolutely cannot," Delia said. "You are four boys, and you will not be running this farm on your own. We have a business to run *together*."

"But you said—" Aaron began.

"Never you mind what I said. Sometimes I get sad, is all, and we will continue working together. But if you four would work a little harder at keeping our home clean, I would appreciate that, too."

"What about Elias?" Moses asked.

The boys all turned toward her, and Delia sighed.

"Elias will be spending time with me, boys," she said.

"And you will not be chasing this man off. I think it's better if we talk about your worries and concerns. And we'll be doing that going forward."

Ezekiel and Thomas exchanged a sly look, and the other two boys looked toward them. There seemed to be an unspoken agreement, and she was relatively certain it was one she wouldn't like.

"Okay, Mamm, if he's going to be coming around, then we will get to know him," Ezekiel said with exaggerated calmness, and Aaron and Thomas both smiled placidly as if they were innocent little lambs. She knew that look—they were trying to fool her.

"We will?" Moses demanded, his gaze snapping fire. "Since when? I don't see why—" Then he let out a yelp. Someone had kicked him under the table, and Ezekiel looked at him meaningfully.

"Of course we will, Moses," Ezekiel said in that same overly calm voice. "Now, let's eat up."

Great. These boys weren't going to let it go that easily, and Elias was in for some trials, she had no doubt. But they'd be going out of their way to hide it from her and to keep her blissfully ignorant. At least Elias wasn't really courting her, and she smiled faintly to herself. She'd make the most of this opportunity, and the next time a man was *really* interested in her hand in marriage, her boys would be ready for it. They thought they were outsmarting her, but it was the other way around. These boys would learn how to talk about their feelings if it was the last thing she did.

Elias shot his mother a smile as she dished up some chicken stew into a bowl. She had gotten smaller and more delicate with age—her hair a soft silver—but her face was nearly unlined. She wasn't as strong as she used to be, and since her cancer treatments, he and his siblings had all gotten a lot more protective of her. That was part of why he could understand Delia's boys' reaction to her dating. He knew what that protective instinct felt like personally.

His father rooted through a box of tools that they'd tried to pack up today. There was always something his *daet* was looking for in their packed boxes.

"Bernard, you should just pretend those boxes don't exist," his mother said. "They are packed. It's done."

"I'm not leaving that door half-fixed," his *daet* replied, but he smiled at his wife all the same. "You knew I was a stickler when you married me, Judith."

His mother laughed at that and shook her head, passing Violet a dish of stew. "At least eat with us, first."

Elias's father came to the table and took his seat at the head. Elias sat down next to him, and Violet across from Elias, and they waited while his mother dished up the last of their bowls before taking a seat herself. They all bowed their heads in silence for a moment and then began to eat.

"So how was your first day of work?" Elias asked his daughter.

"Fine."

"Are you finding it hard?" he asked. Back in Indiana, he worked in a canning plant, and they lived on an acreage. But Violet didn't do much outdoor work besides taking care of the chickens and a bit of kitchen gardening. He hadn't wanted her to start a job like this—hard manual work. He'd rather see her become an excellent cook and seamstress so that she could be ready to find a husband and get married in a few years.

"Not really." Violet took a bite of stew and chewed slowly.

"How do you find working with Delia's sons?" he asked.

She shrugged.

Elias sighed. She wasn't going to say much, it seemed. But she'd been like this for the last year—freezing him out. People said it was normal for that age, but he didn't think it was all just about being a thirteen-year-old girl. Call that a *daet* instinct.

"Those are nice boys," his mother said. "They used to work with their *daet* after school and in the summers, but then Zeke died and they stepped up for their *mamm*. They're hardworking and as polite as I ever saw. They always stop to say hello when they see us, and they're always looking after their *mamm*."

"I've heard that they can be pretty protective of her," Elias said.

"Oh! And that they are!" his father cut in. "Do you know Adel Knussli? She used to be Adel Draschel. Then her husband passed away—Mark, the deacon. You remember him."

"Mark was a few years older than me," Elias said. "But I do remember him being very well-respected, and I was sad to hear of his death. I remember Jacob better, though. We were closer to the same age."

"*Yah*, of course," his father said. "Anyway, Adel was just starting out in matchmaking after Mark's passing and Jacob Knussli needed a wife. There was an inheritance coming, and his uncle had included a stipulation that he be married to get the farm. He had two weeks left before the deadline, and Adel brought him to Delia to meet her and the boys. Even with all that money on the line, it took the boys exactly one visit to chase him off for good!"

Elias's parents exchanged a look and chuckled.

"Adel ended up marrying Jacob herself," his mother added for Violet's benefit. "That's why it's funny."

"Oh." Violet smiled. "Well, good for her."

"And it was for love, might I add," his mother said. "Adel was in knots about it. Jacob was too rebellious for her taste, but she *did* like him."

"But the money softened her up?" Violet asked.

"No, it did not!" Judith retorted. "Marriage is for life—it's a very serious decision. She had to think hard before that commitment. But it worked out. And we're all happy for them."

Elias cast his daughter a rueful smile. She didn't return it.

"Is Adel looking for a match for Delia?" Elias asked, turning to his parents.

"Oh, she's always got her finger in some pie or other," his mother said. "But what her plans are, I don't know. But you could do worse than to go sit down with Adel Knussli, son. She has matched quite a few couples."

"She'd very likely set up a date with Delia," his father added, not taking his eyes off his bowl of stew.

"*Yah*, she likely would," his mother said. "I've pointed it out before, Elias, but Delia is not only a lovely woman—she's your age and a *mamm* already…"

Violet stopped chewing, but she didn't look up.

"We know Delia well," his father added. "She's got good character. And she's a decent cook."

"Not a terrific cook, but middling to good," his mother said with a nod. "You could do worse."

"Is that what we look for in marriage?" Violet asked, looking up. "How well she cooks and if she's already got children? What about feelings?"

"First things first," his mother replied. "You've got to have a foundation."

"On her cooking and children?" Violet shook her head. "Or maybe an inheritance? What about love? What about romance? What about feeling—" she waved a hand in front of her "—I don't know, swept away?"

Elias looked at his daughter in surprise. "Swept away?" Where had she gotten that from?

"Life is about more than duty and meals put on the table!" Violet's voice was taut.

"And you know what life is about?" Elias's father asked gently.

Violet seemed to sense the trap, because she shut her mouth then and looked away.

"Violet, your *mammi* and *dawdie* are just doing what parents do," Elias said. "They're trying to arrange a marriage."

"Is this how you met my *mamm*?" Violet demanded.

He'd told her this story over and over again when Wanda had passed away. It had made him feel better to bring it up and remember how they'd started.

"No, I met her at hymn sing. And we talked a little and I asked to drive her home," he said. "You know the story."

"And you asked her to marry you three weeks later,

and you got married that fall," Violet finished the story. "But didn't you feel anything, Daet? Didn't you fall in love with her and think that you couldn't go another day without her?"

"*Yah*, but I was a much younger man then," he said with a teasing smile. "Now, I'm just tired."

Violet huffed out a sigh. "You're joking, but I'm not, Daet. I don't want someone to marry me because I work hard and I have a good reputation."

"There are worse reasons," Elias's mother murmured.

"This is why I won't marry an Amish man!"

The room suddenly stilled, and her words lodged into Elias's chest.

"I won't!" Violet went on. "I won't marry one! I'm going to marry an Englisher who loves me. And he'll marry me because he thinks I'm his other half, and he'll fall so deeply in love with me that he won't be able to breathe without me."

"That sounds like a medical condition," his father said.

Tears welled in Violet's eyes, and Elias's heart tugged toward her. This was the problem—she saw Englishers as romantic and wonderful, and she thought the Amish life was dull and drab. And Elias didn't know how to fix it.

His father leaned forward. "Dear girl, I don't mean to upset you," he said quietly. "But you are very young, and life is very long. You'll learn that there's value in a good reputation and the ability to work hard. All those fluttery feelings are as permanent as butterflies. What remains is what lasts."

"Well, I don't want that!" Violet's eyes flashed. "I

don't want duty and responsibility. I want romance and love and…and…" She pushed her bowl away angrily.

"You want an Englisher," Elias concluded dully.

"*Yah*, I do." Violet looked around the table, defiance in those blue eyes. "I won't waste my life."

Had this gone further than Elias thought? She was so young—it was like yesterday that she was a bouncing little girl with a lisp. And now she was just a step from womanhood, declaring that Amish life wasn't for her. Young people changed their minds about their extreme opinions, didn't they? This couldn't stick!

"Do you think there is no love or satisfaction in our Amish life?" Elias asked.

"I think there is love, but I want more than just love. I want *romance*," she replied.

Where was she getting these ideas from? There was plenty of romance in Amish marriages! But all she'd seen the last while was sadness and grief. He'd thought he was protecting her by holding off on finding a new wife. And maybe he was protecting himself…but now he had a teenage daughter who thought that the life of stable, devoted responsibility was boring. She should be so blessed as to find a stable and devoted husband one day!

"And you think there is no romance in a man choosing a good woman and getting to know her in a chaste and Christian way?" Elias asked.

Violet gave him a long-suffering look that told him all he needed to know.

"Well, then, I'll tell you what," Elias said. "I'm going to prove you wrong."

"How?" his parents asked at once.

"*Yah*, how?" Violet asked.

"I'm going to get to know Delia next door. I'm going to take her out for a drive, and I'm going to talk to her about serious things. And you will see that Amish people are perfectly capable of all the romance you can imagine."

Violet blinked at him. "You're going to take my *boss* out driving?"

Elias nodded. "*Yah*, if she'll go with me."

And considering their talk earlier, he was rather confident that she would. Even if they just sat in the buggy and talked about their parenting challenges. And truthfully, that sounded like an awfully nice evening to him about now.

"Well!" his mother said with a smile. "That is nice."

"You could do worse," his father said with a nod.

"Dawdie, that is not romantic at all!" Violet said. "He's only doing it to try and make a point! Do you really think my father toying with the feelings of the woman next door is a good idea?"

"I can't rightfully say why your father is doing this," his father said with the tickle of a smile at the corners of his lips. "But a wise man always says half of what he feels and a quarter of what he thinks, and he has fewer words to eat later."

"What does that mean?" Violet asked.

"It means I'm going to shut my mouth and let your father ask a nice woman out for driving. We'll see how it goes."

Violet pressed her lips together. "I suppose we will."

"It will go wonderfully!" His mother beamed. "I just know it."

Great. Now his parents were invested in this—his

mother, at least. Thankfully his father took more to convince about things like love and marriage. But his daughter?

Maybe after seeing Elias court Delia, she would be able to see herself finding a nice Amish man of her own. Maybe Violet needed proof that there was still life, love, and something to live for in the Amish community.

# *Chapter Three*

The next morning, Delia stood at the bottom of the stairs. She had a pile of pancakes waiting in the oven, some fried potatoes on the stovetop, some sausages fried and a big bowl of boiled eggs waiting on the kitchen table. She could hear her sons' footfalls and chatter overhead.

"And bring down all your laundry!" she called. "I'm doing laundry today, and I want it all sorted into piles in the basement!"

Four boys working outdoors made for a constant pile of dirt-crusted laundry. Most women in the county did their laundry on Mondays, but Delia didn't have a husband working the farm, so she did the laundry whenever she could squeeze it in. Today, Wednesday, would just have to do. And with Violet working outside—hopefully her good attitude would remain intact—Delia was taking advantage of a morning at the wringer washer in the basement.

Aaron and Thomas came down first, their laundry baskets filled to overflowing.

"You know how it goes," Delia said. "Whites in one pile, colored shirts and socks and whatnot in another pile, and your pants in a third pile."

*"Yah, yah..."* Aaron said, and they plodded past her toward the basement stairs.

"And good morning!" she sang after them.

Thomas grunted, and Delia turned back to getting breakfast onto the table. Moses was the next one down the stairs, struggling with his basket of dirty clothes.

"Good morning, Moses," she said.

"Morning, Mamm."

"Is that all of your dirty clothes?" Delia asked.

*"Yah."*

"Will I find any socks or shirts behind your door?"

"No." But he stopped on the staircase.

"Are you sure?"

Moses turned around and headed back up. *Yah*, that was what she thought. Aaron and Thomas came back up from the basement, and Ezekiel Jr. came down the stairs with his own hamper. She never had to check up on Ezekiel. His side of the room he shared with Thomas would be neat and clean, and his clothes would be hung up and put away. The minute he'd started dating a girl in the community, he'd suddenly gotten more responsible and neat. He never wanted Beulah to catch him looking rumpled.

Delia got the plates to set the table and snagged a jug of syrup on her way past. When Ezekiel was coming up from the basement, Moses was headed back down the stairs again.

"Hurry up, Moses," Aaron said. "We're hungry."

"I'm hungry, too!" Moses retorted.

"Hurry up, then," Thomas said.

"Here—pass me your hamper," Ezekiel said, and he took the clothes hamper from his brother. "Go sit down."

Ezekiel was a little bossy, but he did streamline things around the home, and he trotted down the basement stairs, returning a couple of minutes later with a pair of suspenders in one hand. He handed them over to Moses, whose face went red. Moses was at a sensitive age, and he was easily embarrassed.

"Okay, boys, let's say grace before the food gets cold," Delia said, and they all bowed their heads.

The boys ate quickly, and it seemed that their earnestness about helping out more from the night before hadn't faded away, as she'd expected. They finished eating, and Ezekiel started barking orders.

"Moses, clear the table. Aaron, you start washing dishes, and Thomas—you dry. I'm going to sweep the kitchen," Ezekiel said. "Then we all head out and clean the stable together—it'll be quicker that way, and Mamm won't have to clean up after us like a bunch of babies."

"Thank you, boys," Delia said. "I appreciate this."

They got to work with a lot more clatter and banging than she would have liked, but she wasn't about to say anything to stop this wonderful display of helpfulness. Delia went down to the basement to start the water filling into the wringer washer, and when she heard a knock, she came back upstairs.

Ezekiel was just letting Violet and Elias into the house.

"Morning, Elias," Ezekiel said brusquely, sounding a little too much like he thought himself an equal, to Delia's ear.

"Good morning!" she called, trying to offset her son's sternness.

Elias smiled, and Violet glanced between them uneasily. Had he dropped the news on his daughter that he'd be "courting"?

"I thought I'd come by and say hello, since Violet was coming to start work."

Elias shot her a conspiratorial smile, and she found herself smiling back. This might be fun…pretending to be something more than they were. She did miss having some male company. Men were different than women when chatting in a kitchen. They saw the world differently, and she missed having a grown man to discuss things with— more than she'd realized.

"That's very nice," Delia said. "I'm glad you did. My boys are just finishing up a few chores, and if you'd like some coffee, I was about to start some."

"Coffee would be great," he said with a nod.

"I could even whip up a fresh batch of muffins. The *kinner* will need some snack food later, as it is," she said.

"Mamm, you don't have to do that," Thomas interjected from the sink where he and Aaron were doing the dishes. "There's plenty of leftovers. Plus the dry bread. We'll make milky tea and dip bread in it."

"*Yah*, that's what we'll have," Aaron agreed quickly.

"I like muffins—" Moses started and was knocked between the shoulder blades by Ezekiel's broom. "Oh, I mean, I don't want them."

Delia rolled her eyes. "Boys, I love you all so much, but you need to focus on your own work and let me plan my own day."

Ezekiel finished filling a dustpan, then put the broom away in a cupboard. He crossed his arms over his chest and eyed Elias. She'd made it clear the night before that she'd be spending some time with Elias, and now she could see how her sons were going to react to that.

"Sorry, Mamm," Ezekiel said. "We just don't want to make more work for you. You work hard enough as it is."

"And I've survived this long," Delia said. "You're very sweet to worry about how hard I work, but I want muffins to snack on for myself, too."

Ezekiel smiled a little bashfully, and her heart gave a tumble. These boys could do that so easily!

"Nice day out there," Ezekiel said, turning to Elias.

"*Yah*, very nice," Elias agreed. "How is my daughter doing with her job?"

Elias looked fixedly at Ezekiel, not at Delia, and she waited for her son to answer.

"She's doing all right. She's learning as she goes," Ezekiel said.

"You're not working her too hard?" Elias asked.

"The work is as hard as it is," Ezekiel replied. "It's outdoor work. If she wants the job, she has to do it. If she doesn't want the job, we'll do it ourselves. That's how this works."

"Ezekiel!" Delia said. "You're speaking with Violet's *daet*. I'd expect more manners than that."

"No, it's okay," Elias said. "He's just saying it like it is, and I appreciate that, especially where it concerns my daughter." He glanced over at Violet. "Are you up for it?"

"I said before I could do it," Violet said testily.

"I won't let her get hurt," Ezekiel said. "I know what needs to be done, but like I said, she doesn't need to be the one to do it. If she's in over her head, I'll send her home. Simple as that."

Delia threw up her hands. It was like this boy had been raised in a barn!

"You aren't allowed to do that!" Violet spoke up. "Is he?"

"I am, and I would," Ezekiel retorted. "What is this to you, anyway? It's just a job. You can just as easily babysit, or help my *mamm* here in the house."

"Ezekiel, she wants to work outdoors," Delia cut in. "Give her a chance, would you?"

She met her son's gaze. The truth was, if Ezekiel sent the girl home, she'd back him up. Her son was nearly grown, and he knew the work, and they didn't have time to have mistakes out there. Not at this time of year.

"*Yah*, I said I would, Mamm," Ezekiel said. "But Elias here seems worried about her doing the job."

"*Are* you worried?" Violet asked, turning to face her father.

"A little," he said. "But if Ezekiel will make sure you're not overworked, then I'll trust that. For today."

"Daet—" Violet started, and then she shook her head. "Fine. Let me prove it to you again today. I'm not over-worked."

"Okay," he said. "Fair enough."

"It's okay, Violet," Delia said. "*Daets* can be a little overprotective. That's all. You were a great help yester-day. And Elias, I'm not going to let her get overtired, either. Trust me—I have a good sense of these things. I'll keep an eye on her."

Elias did relax a little then, but Ezekiel didn't.

"Maybe you want to come see the work your daughter is doing. I could show you, myself," Ezekiel suggested, and he glanced over at Delia. He was trying to get Elias outside so he could talk to him alone, and she knew it.

"I think you should show him, Ezekiel—*after a coffee*," Delia said firmly. "We are old friends, and we need to catch up. Then you can show him the jobs Violet will be doing."

Ezekiel pressed his lips together. He wouldn't openly defy her, especially not in front of Elias. Her eldest son glanced at his brothers, who were now finished their chores and were watching the scene with interest.

"All right," Ezekiel said. "Let's get to work, guys... and Violet."

Violet shot Ezekiel a brilliant smile. "Let's."

Sometimes Delia forgot what handsome boys she had, and Ezekiel was considered quite good-looking by the girls around here. The boys headed out of the house, but not without each of them giving Elias a pointed look on his way past.

"I'll put together some snacks for you if you want to come grab something later on," Delia called after them.

The boys went into the mudroom, and there was the sound of boots stomping as they put them on, and the bass of the older boys' voices mingled with Moses's higher voice. Violet stood back and watched them in silence, and when the screen door banged, and there was room in the mudroom, she went in to get her own boots back on.

"Don't forget the work apron, Violet!" Delia called after her.

"I've got it!" Violet called back, and the screen door banged again.

The sound of boots on the steps echoed back into the

house, and then all was still. Delia felt some heat in her cheeks as she faced Elias for the first time alone since they had discussed their pretend courtship. He was a rather handsome man—tall, muscular, lean—and his beard was a glossy, dark brown. She knew their arrangement was pretend, but it did seem to change things between them, and she suddenly found herself uncertain of what to say.

So she turned around and headed for the stove to start the promised coffee.

"Did you tell your boys you'll be seeing more of me?" Elias asked.

"*Yah*, I did," she said. "And when you go see Violet's work, Ezekiel and the older ones will posture a bit. Be warned."

She glanced back over her shoulder as she filled the coffee percolator. She headed out to the summer cooking porch and put it onto the stove. She stoked up the fire, and came back inside with perspiration beading her forehead.

"I know this is all for show," Elias said, "but I am going to enjoy this—some good cooking and conversation with someone who understands."

She felt her shoulders relax and she smiled. "You do know the *kinner* will try and outsmart us."

"Of course," he replied. "I would expect nothing less."

Delia's eyes crinkled up when she laughed, and Elias was suddenly struck by just how pretty she was. Her hair had a whisper of gray woven through her dark tresses, pulled back into a voluminous bun at the back of her head. Her hair would be very long, and he remembered what it was like when his wife used to wash her hair and let it hang loose down her back to let it dry. Delia's hair would be down to her knees, almost. He shouldn't be thinking such things. Unless he was her husband, her hair was not his business. He dropped his gaze. This wasn't going to work if he actually fell for her, would it? What he needed right now was a friend, not a serious complication.

"The boys reacted the way I thought they would," Delia said. "There was a lot of argument about you using me to get the farm, and how I didn't need a man around here because they'd pick up the extra slack."

He smiled at that. "They think that a husband is only about the outdoor work? Nothing more?"

"They seem to."

"That's...sweet. Innocent."

"They are all of them sweet and innocent," she agreed. "But they won't be easy on you."

"That's why it's a good thing I'm not really courting you," he said. "They can't offend me, Delia. Don't worry about it."

Well, maybe they could offend him just a little. Teenagers had a bull's-eye ability to find a man's weaknesses, and they didn't have the maturity to show any restraint. But he'd brush it off. He was the adult, after all.

"And what about Violet?" Delia asked.

"She thought that me getting to know you was entirely unromantic," he said. "My parents suggested that you were a woman of character and might be good for me."

"No!" She shot him a joking grin. "And that wasn't romantic for her?"

"No, she wanted hearts being cast about, and...I don't

know what all. She doesn't like the pragmatic approach to a relationship—two people looking for certain qualities first, and then looking for a connection after that. She thinks people should fall madly in love with each other and think about other things later, I suppose."

Delia chuckled. "There's nothing wrong with some pragmatism. It's part of Amish life."

It was part of Amish life, and he couldn't imagine that intelligent Englishers behaved so very differently. What was the use in letting yourself fall in love with a woman when it just wouldn't work?

"But Violet figures she'll find her wild romance with an Englisher man."

Delia's smile faded. "Oh, Elias... She said that?"

"*Yah.* In so many words." He paused. "You were thirteen once. If you'd said something like that, would you have meant it?"

She nodded. "I don't think a girl that age says too much she doesn't mean in the moment. But she can still gain some wisdom, change her mind."

"That's my hope," he said, and his heart gave a little twist. "She's my only child, Delia. And a daughter, to boot. To think of her leaving us, and throwing herself away on some man outside our faith..."

"She'll want a good man," Delia said softly. "And she's not old enough to look for one anyway. There's time before her *Rumspringa*. Gott has his ways of getting through to us—people she'll meet, examples she'll see of other girls making the wrong choice or just some advice that finally lands on fruitful soil."

"I don't want her to be the example to others about what to avoid," he said gruffly.

"I agree. And she really thought that you getting to know me wasn't romantic in the least?"

He smiled ruefully, then. "I thought it was, at least. Come on, two people who've lost as much as we have getting to know each other better, thinking about a future—that's romance all over it."

Delia rolled her eyes. "And since when is it unromantic to look at things reasonably before offering your heart?" she asked. "Hearts are much more vulnerable than young people ever dream. They get broken, shattered, damaged... A heart is not to be toyed with, and an unworthy man can completely break a woman!"

"You said it better than I did," he replied.

"But she's thirteen and she longs for romance..." Delia frowned slightly. "Sometimes we work so hard to keep privacy between a man and wife that I think we do our *kinner* a disservice. They need to see adults happy and in love."

But their culture didn't lend itself to public displays of affection, and Elias was glad of that. He was a more reticent kind of man—the kind who might feel deeply but didn't want others to see it.

"I should probably warn you that my mother is quite thrilled at the thought of you and I exploring a future," he added.

Some color touched her cheeks. "I do feel a bit bad about disappointing Judith. She's such a treasure."

"She feels the same way about you." He shrugged. "But she'll be okay. I think the ends justify the means this once."

"So do I, actually," Delia said. "At the end of this, our

*kinner* will be ready to take a step forward. And we'll have helped them get there."

Delia went out onto the cooking porch again. She came back a moment later with the hot coffeepot, and Elias headed over to the cupboards.

"Where are the mugs?" he asked.

"That upper cupboard—you're right in front of it."

Elias grabbed two white coffee mugs and brought them back to the table. He stopped by the kitchen window and looked outside. He could see his daughter dragging a hose toward a flower garden, and the tallest of Delia's boys was giving some instructions, waving one hand about as he gestured toward the rows. She was nodding cooperatively—a rather pleasant side to his daughter he hadn't been seeing a lot in her lately. Maybe this job would be good for her, after all.

"So, I figured that it might be nice for us to do something traditional—something that will look like obvious courting to our *kinner*," Elias said.

"Oh?"

"I wanted to take you on a buggy ride tonight," he said.

"A buggy ride!" She smiled at that. "That does sound very official. People will talk."

"Do you mind?" he asked.

Because up until this point, they'd been considering how their *kinner* would react. But their going out in a buggy together would interest the whole community. There would be gossip—no doubt about that.

Delia filled both their mugs and then put down the coffeepot wordlessly.

"If it's too much—" he started.

"I don't think I do mind," she said at last. "There has

been a lot of pity, and I told you before that I don't want to be 'Poor Delia' anymore. Let them think of me as Delia-who's-looking-for-a-husband. I think I'd rather that, anyway."

"So…is that a yes?" he asked. "You'll let me take you driving this evening?"

*"Yah."* She nodded, and her eyes sparkled into a smile. "You have yourself a date, Elias. And you might not want to worry so much about what people will say about me… You'll be fielding questions from everyone come Service Sunday!"

Elias chuckled. "You're right. I probably will be."

But all the same, he couldn't help but feel a surge of victory. She'd agreed to go driving with him.

"How do you like your coffee?" Delia asked, and she nudged cream and a bottle of milk across the table toward him.

"Black," he said, and he took a sip. He liked his coffee like he liked the rest of his life—uncomplicated and straightforward. But he was complicating everything, wasn't he? "I won't keep you long. I know you've got things to do, and I've promised your son that I'll take a look at my daughter's work."

"Oh, don't worry about Ezekiel," she said.

"On the contrary," he replied. "Ezekiel is the ringleader here. He knows what he wants for his *mamm*, and I doubt that the man who will please Ezekiel walks this green earth. If Ezekiel doesn't make his peace with you moving on, you'll never get your boys to relax."

"You might be right," she said.

"So I'm going to keep my word to that boy, and I'm

going to talk to him. I have a feeling he'll say more to me than he will to you right now. It's a man thing."

They finished their coffee, and then Delia mentioned that she had laundry to do, which was Elias's cue to let her get to her housework.

"I'll pick you up tonight at seven, if that's okay," he said.

"I'll be ready." She shot him a smile.

And he almost felt like a teenager again himself, planning a date that would cause nothing but drama behind their backs. And there was satisfaction in that.

If Violet wanted romance and drama, she was about to witness a doozy!

Once outside, Elias spotted Ezekiel coming out of the stable, pulling off his gloves and tucking them under one suspender. Elias waved at him, and Ezekiel came over.

"She's watering some plants right now," Ezekiel said, nodding in Violet's direction.

"*Yah*, I noticed that," Elias said. "And I'm sure she'll be fine under your watch."

Ezekiel straightened just a little at the implied compliment.

"I wanted to let you know that I'm taking your *mamm* out driving this evening," Elias said.

"*Yah?*" Ezekiel's tone cooled.

"*Yah.* I know your *mamm* from years ago, and we used to be friends," he said. "It's nice to get to know her again."

"Getting to know her again can happen with that coffee inside, not in a buggy," Ezekiel retorted. He sounded like a scolding father.

"We don't need permission," Elias said pointedly.

Ezekiel nodded twice and pressed his lips together. "My *mamm* isn't just some woman in need of a man about the place, you know."

"I know that."

"This land will come to my brothers and me. It won't be yours."

"That's fine by me."

Ezekiel's jaw rippled as he clenched his teeth, but he didn't say anything. He kicked at a stone in the dirt, sending it skittering into the grass.

"Just say it," Elias said. "You know you want to."

Ezekiel looked like he might think better of it, but then he nodded curtly.

"Okay, then I will. She's soft," Ezekiel said, his quiet tone contrasting with the fire in his eyes. "Our *mamm* is gentle and kind and funny and… She's special, and while she has it all under control, you could hurt her."

"You think—" Elias started.

"No, listen," Ezekiel snapped. "Mamm has been through a lot, and we've chased off better men than you."

"I heard," he replied. "But your mother is her own woman. And she deserves a future with another husband, if that's what she chooses."

"Our *daet* isn't that easy to replace," Ezekiel replied. "We know what our *mamm* is worth, and making her laugh for a little while isn't enough. Not for us. You might charm our mother, but she won't marry a man we don't approve. And—" Ezekiel looked him up and down "—we don't approve."

"She's your mother," Elias said. "She deserves your respect."

"She *has* my respect," Ezekiel retorted. "So I'll say

this—if my mother sheds so much as one tear over you, I'll make it my personal business to see you pay for it."

Elias blinked at the young man. He'd hoped for honesty, but he hadn't expected a threat.

"I won't hurt her, Ezekiel," Elias said. Far from it. Delia's heart was safe from him—the *kinner* just didn't know it.

"See that you don't," Ezekiel replied. "Mark my words. You will pay for every tear."

Ezekiel turned and stalked off in the direction of the gardens, and Elias watched him go. This was going to be harder than he thought. But he'd get that young man's trust yet.

Delia deserved her freedom, even from the devoted love of her own children.

## Chapter Four

"You're going on a buggy ride with Elias Lehman?" Thomas asked, folding his arms over his chest. "Like… like Ezekiel and Beulah?"

Delia stood at the counter, arranging some cut flowers into a bouquet on a square of brown paper. She tucked some baby's breath in behind the lilies and fragrant, fully open peach-colored rose blooms. They wouldn't last long in a vase, but they would be beautiful.

"Not entirely like that," Delia replied. "We're going to stop by the Speichers' place. Willa has been sick, and I want to bring her some flowers to cheer her up. She loves our roses."

"That's it?" Thomas asked with a frown. "You don't need Elias to drive you there. If you want company, one of us would go with you."

"I can go along," Moses piped up. He rubbed a hand over his freckled nose.

The boys stood in the kitchen, the dishes washed and mostly put away.

"It's obviously more than just a visit with neighbors," Ezekiel said. "Elias told me he wanted to take you out for a ride tonight."

"That's a date, Mamm," Aaron said. "Even I know that. When a man asks you to go riding in his buggy, that's a date."

As if Delia needed schooling on how people courted! It was mildly annoying how naive her own boys seemed to think she was.

"I'm well aware that it's a date," Delia said. "But I can do more than one thing at once, and I want to bring these flowers to Willa." She wrapped the bottom of the cut flowers with a wet piece of paper towel, and then folded the paper over the bouquet and tied the middle with a piece of twine. "And this is not up for debate. I'm sure you'll be fine without me for a couple of hours."

"And if we don't like him?" Moses asked.

"Then I suggest you learn to like him," Delia replied. "He's a very nice man, and you boys need to learn that you aren't the men in this home."

"Then what are we?" Thomas demanded.

"You are the children," she said. "You are the growing, maturing, responsible and wonderful children whom I am very proud of. But you are still the children. I am your *mamm*, and I make the rules. You don't get to be rude to my guests." She looked around at her sons pointedly.

"He isn't just a guest, though, is he?" Ezekiel asked. "If he's interested in you, you'd think he'd want to get to know your children, too."

"Ezekiel," she said, pinning her eldest son with a no-nonsense look. "When you started taking Beulah out, did you start by getting to know her brothers and sisters and parents first? Or did you start with Beulah? When you decided that Beulah really was a wonderful girl and that she returned your feelings, then you spent more time with her family. Am I right?"

"Fine, you're right," he grudgingly agreed.

"And what about me? I need time to get to know Elias, too. What if I decide I'm not interested after all? You act as if I'm a potted plant to be picked up and carried off at will. Well, I'm not. And I have to get to know him better, too. I think you'd better trust my ability to judge character."

"You might not see what we see," Thomas said.

"I raised four good boys," Delia said. "Give me a little bit of credit for knowing what's decent and what isn't, would you?"

Delia could hear the sound of hooves and buggy wheels outside, and she went to the window and looked out. Elias reined in his horse and then hopped down from the buggy. He spotted her in the window and waved.

"He's here," Delia said brightly. "Now, I expect this kitchen to be clean when I get back. And don't forget to shine the church shoes, Moses. This weekend is Service Sunday, and we have to be ready."

Delia didn't wait for argument, but her heart did squeeze a little at the silence behind her. She looked back once as she opened the door, the paper-wrapped flowers in one arm. Her sons all stared at her, mute and shocked.

"We'll talk about all of our feelings when I get back," she said.

"Our feelings?" Thomas asked weakly.

"Yes. Our feelings. Yours and mine."

They'd hate that, she knew, but it was high time they learned that skill. Some men only figured it out once they were married. Some discovered the skill when they were courting. Girls had a way of getting a boy to talk. But her sons needed to be able to talk in this family—now!

She pulled the door shut firmly behind her, and as she walked toward the buggy, she heard the boys from inside, their voices suddenly erupting as they complained to each other. She smothered a smile.

Elias waited beside the buggy, leaning against it with his arms crossed. He looked over her shoulder toward the house, and she glanced back to see Thomas and Moses in the window. When they saw her looking at them, they disappeared.

"How'd they take you leaving with me?" Elias asked.

"I didn't give them a chance to argue," she said. "I'm their mother. I'm going out. They'll survive."

Elias grinned. "I agree. Flowers? Should I have brought you some?"

"No, these are for Willa Speicher," Delia said. "I wanted to stop by and bring her something to cheer her up. She's been sick for weeks with that terrible flu that got into her lungs."

Elias held out his hand and she allowed him to boost her up into the buggy. His grip was firm, and she couldn't help the way her stomach fluttered at his strong, helping hand. She settled into the passenger-side seat, and Elias hoisted himself up next to her, his arm settling next to hers. He was warm, and he smelled like soap.

Elias flicked the reins and he turned the horse around. Delia leaned forward to look toward the house again. The side door was open and Moses stood in the doorway, watching her with wide eyes.

"Oh, that's some powerful guilt," Elias said. "They are pulling out all the stops, aren't they?"

"I'm starting to feel bad," she said.

"Don't." Elias chuckled. "We're going for a drive. We'll bring flowers to a sick lady, and I'll drop you back off at home. You're doing nothing wrong, Delia."

And she knew that. Even if this *was* a real date, it wouldn't be wrong, but her boys were fighting this courting with everything in their arsenal.

"How did Violet handle you taking me out for a drive?" Delia asked.

"She's sulking," he replied. "She said she wasn't hungry for dinner and went upstairs."

"Did you talk to her?" Delia asked.

"She told me to go away, and my mother assured me that she'll have a chat with her while I'm gone," he replied. His voice was calm and relaxed, but she noticed how his hands tightened on the reins.

"It's terrible when they punish us, isn't it?" she said, nudging his arm with hers.

Elias looked over at her and a smile crinkled around his eyes. "*Yah.* I hate it. She gives me this look that she's used on me since she was three years old. And Wanda used to laugh and say that I was wrapped around her finger."

"Zeke used to say that I was the soft touch, too," Delia said. "He said I had to learn to stick to my orders with them. And he was right. These last two years without him, I've had to get firmer with the boys to keep control. I can't tell them that their father will have a word with them when they act up anymore, now, can I?"

"You seem to have a pretty good handle on your home, though," Elias said.

"Do I? Thank you for that."

"*Yah.* They're polite, well-raised boys. They work hard, they're dedicated, and they're a credit to you."

That felt good to hear. "Your Violet is a good girl, too. She's been keeping up with the boys, and that's not easy, especially considering this is her first job."

The horse pulled the buggy out onto the road, and Elias flicked the reins and they sped up to a trot. The breeze that came into the buggy was cooling against her face and neck.

"But we still feel a little guilty, don't we?" she asked.

"We are the parents, and they are the *kinner.*"

"True enough… But it makes me feel better that I'm not the only one whose *kinner* are giving her a hard time."

"You aren't alone in that," he replied with a low laugh. "I'm glad we can do this without the pressure of an actual courtship. I've been worried that when I do decide to marry again, Violet will scare off any potential stepmother. This is a difficult age."

"After this experiment, she might be ready to accept a nice woman in your life," Delia replied, and for a fleeting second, she felt a little stab of envy for the woman who'd get Elias's true and honest attention focused on her.

"I hope so…" Elias was quiet, and the silence was filled with the clopping rhythm of horse hooves. "I don't remember how to get to the Speichers' place."

"Up here at the stop sign, you turn left," she said.

The Speicher acreage was a twenty-five minute drive

from Delia's flower farm. Art and Willa Speicher had been retired for some time—Art had worked at a factory for thirty years before he retired—and they shared a house with their youngest daughter, Lydia. Willa's health had not been good the last little while.

When they turned into the drive, Art was out in the front flower garden weeding, and Willa was on the porch with a blanket over her legs and a mug between her hands. She looked smaller and frailer than Delia had ever seen her. But more surprising than Willa's frail state was the fact that an Englisher teenage boy was kneeling at the other end of the garden with an ice cream bucket full of weeds, too. A little red sedan—also definitely out of place—was parked out by the buggy shelter.

Lydia appeared at the side door, an apron over her dress and kitchen towel over one shoulder. She was a slim woman with large brown eyes. She waved at Delia and gave her a curious look. *Yah*, Lydia would have questions about Elias, that was for sure and certain.

"Good evening, Delia!" Art called, pushing himself to his feet. "And is that…Elias Lehman? Is that you?"

"*Yah*, *yah*, it's me, all right," Elias said.

Delia got down from the buggy, and Elias hopped down on his side. Delia cast Elias a smile and headed up to the porch with her wrapped flowers. The men would chat and catch up, and she'd have a moment with Willa and Lydia. She sent a smile in the teenager's direction, too. He looked to be about Thomas's or Aaron's age. He had the same gangly, angular look of a teenager still growing into his limbs. Her heart immediately softened at the sight of him.

"Have you met my grandson?" Willa called. "This is Liam—Paul's son."

That made sense. Willa and Art's oldest son, Paul, had gone English years ago, but he had left the community before he was baptized, so he wasn't shunned. Delia waved at the young man.

"Hello, Liam," she said. "It's nice to meet you. Are you here for a visit?"

"Hi. Yeah, just visiting," Liam said, pushing himself up from his weeding and wiping the dirt off the knees of his jeans. The light was getting low, the sun near setting. "Mammi, I'm just going to get a drink."

"Of course, dear," Willa said, and she coughed into a handkerchief.

Liam slipped past Delia and headed into the house just as Lydia came outside.

"It's nice to see you," Lydia said.

Willa accepted the flowers and unwrapped them. "Oh, Delia, these are gorgeous. Thank you!" She coughed again, hunching over the handkerchief. "I'm sorry, I'm still getting over the last of the pneumonia, the doctor says. But fresh air is supposed to be good for me."

"You've met Liam?" Lydia asked.

"*Yah*, barely," Delia replied. "He looks to be what… fourteen, fifteen?"

"Sixteen," Lydia clarified, then she lowered her voice. "My brother sent him to spend some time here since he'd been getting into trouble a lot at school."

"Oh, dear…" Delia winced. "Well, some fresh air and sunshine might do him some good, too."

"That's the hope," Willa murmured.

"Let me take those." Lydia reached for the flowers in

her mother's hands, then her gaze moved across the grass toward where the men stood. "Is that Elias Lehman?"

"*Yah*. I hardly recognized him yesterday when we met. He's helping his parents move. I've hired his daughter to help out at the flower farm."

"Are you..." Lydia licked her lips. "Are you...getting to know him?"

"*Yah*. Well, a little. I mean—it isn't serious. It's—" She swallowed hastily. "We have *kinner* the same age, you see. And we understand what that's like, and..."

"Now, now," Willa said, putting a cool hand over Delia's. "You're both grown. If you want to get to know a widower, that is entirely your business. You aren't a teenager in your *Rumspringa*!"

"In fact, I have a boy of my own in his *Rumspringa*," Delia said, attempting to joke.

"How are the boys doing?" Willa asked.

The conversation turned toward Ezekiel's new buggy that she'd put a down payment on, and the calves Aaron and Thomas wanted to raise for market. Lydia was a talented knitter and crocheter, and she was trying her hand at some knit sweaters to sell at a local shop in town.

Liam emerged from the house with a glass of iced tea.

"Where do you live, Liam?" Delia asked.

"Pittsburgh."

"So this must be very different than what you're used to," she said.

"I guess. Yeah. No TV or internet, except what I can get on my phone. And I have to charge it in the neighbor's barn."

Delia chuckled. "That's true. But there's so much

more to do out here, don't you think? There's horses and cattle and always a job to do."

Liam shrugged. "A lot of work. That's why my dad sent me out here—to work."

Right. Punishment, probably, for his misbehavior during the school year. She'd have a few consequences for her own boys if they decided to act up and get into trouble, too. She could only respect proactive parents who did their best to straighten out their misbehaving *kinner*.

"There is a youth event coming up Monday evening," Delia said. "My *kinner* are all going—I have boys your age. It's a volleyball tournament at the Lapp farm. All the young people will be there."

"Yeah?" Liam brightened. "There's like…teenagers? And fun?"

"*Yah*, we have teenagers here," Delia chuckled. "And if you like volleyball and food and standing around talking, then you'll have a good time. Talk to your grandparents about it. It might be nice to see some people your own age."

Willa raised her eyebrows and glanced in the direction of her husband. "That's an idea, isn't it?"

But her comment didn't confirm whether or not the boy would be permitted to go. Willa started to cough again, and she took a sip of her hot tea.

"I'm sorry, Delia, but I think I'm going to go inside and lay down," Willa said, and she took another sip of tea.

"Of course, Willa," Delia said. "I just wanted to come by and tell you that we're praying for you and bring you those roses since they reminded me of you."

"Thank you, dear…" And she leaned over to cough again.

It was time to get going. Poor Willa needed some rest, and there were times when friends were not the medicine that a sick person needed most. Delia came down the steps and let Lydia help her mother to her feet.

"Goodbye!" Lydia said. "We'll have to get together for a proper chat one of these days."

"We sure will," Delia replied. "Take care!"

Elias held out his hand and helped Delia up into the buggy. She was a few inches shorter than him, and he liked the feel of her hand in his. He caught the look of obvious surprise on Art's face when he did so, and Elias felt his face heat. *Yah*, he knew how it looked—it was supposed to look that way! And there was no shame in two people who had lost their spouses exploring a possible romance. In fact, in Amish communities this was encouraged. But he still felt a little caught out, as if he was a teenager again and all eyes were on him.

He got up into the buggy next to Delia, and she sent him a smile that lowered his blood pressure just a bit. She seemed to have a calming effect on him.

"Their grandson is visiting for a few weeks," Delia said. "He's Paul's son. Do you remember Paul?"

"*Yah*, I remember when he jumped the fence," Elias replied. "That was the summer before I left for Indiana. I remember how crushed his parents were. Willa sat in our kitchen and sobbed her heart out while my *mamm* did her best to comfort her."

Elias flicked the reins and they started forward, pulling around to go back up the drive. He looked out the window and saw Art and his grandson standing there watching them go. He waved, and they waved back.

"My *mamm* sat us all down and talked to us about the dangers out there," Delia said. "It scared all the parents, because Paul was a nice boy."

"Well… Paul talked a lot about leaving," Elias said. "We weren't very close friends, but we saw each other at all the youth group events. He wanted to be a car mechanic. All us boys knew that."

"I thought he was just talking big," Delia said. "He's the first one I knew who actually left."

"For weeks, we just waited, figuring he'd come back," Elias added. "Do you remember how we prayed for his return in youth group?"

Delia nodded mutely. The entire community had been shaken up when Paul left, and Elias remembered still thinking he'd come back a year later when Elias was leaving for work in Indiana.

"It's a good warning that teenagers will often do just what they say in anger," Elias said quietly. And Violet was saying a lot in anger lately. As her father, he was taking her threats incredibly seriously.

Elias leaned forward, waiting until a car passed before he flicked the reins and they pulled back out onto the road. He caught a glimpse of Delia in the corner of his eye, and she looked so calm and pretty sitting there, her dark brown eyes focused on the road ahead.

"Ironically, Paul sent his son back to Amish Country for the summer because he was getting in trouble in school," Delia said. "It seems that Paul still turns to Amish ways when things get hard out there with the Englishers."

"*Yah*, it seems so," Elias agreed. "Sending his son to his parents is the right thing for him to do, too. It's safe here—people have values and morals. That boy will see a different way to live. Maybe he'll become Amish."

"I'm not sure about that," Delia replied. "He was talking about having no TV or internet. That can be hard for them."

"Hmm." Wouldn't it be nice if the boy did come to the Amish faith, though? The horse's hooves clopped merrily along the pavement, and Elias pushed his hat back on his head to let some breeze reach his forehead.

"Liam reminds me of my boys," Delia said. "Maybe it's just the age. He's sixteen. They think they're so grown-up, and they try to sound so adult, but really they are just very large *kinner* at that age."

Elias shot her a wry smile. "You see the boy in him."

"I'm a *mamm*. I can't help it."

"I like that about you," he said.

"That I'm a mother?" she asked, looking mildly surprised.

"*Yah.*" He shrugged. "I know that seems simple, but I really do. There were some women in my community in Indiana who were interested in pursuing more with me, but they didn't have *kinner* of their own, and…and I think they saw Violet as a problem to solve instead of a girl to love."

"Ah." Delia nodded. "*Yah*, those are considerations I have with courting, too. My *daet* died when I was a teenager, and my *mamm* remarried."

"I didn't realize that," Elias said. "Your *mamm* and *daet*—I suppose your step*daet*—seemed like they'd been together forever. I never even questioned it."

She was silent.

"Was it a good experience at home?" he asked cautiously.

"Not really." She winced. "We kept up good appearances, but I always knew that my stepfather had married my mother because he loved her, and he'd gotten us as part of the package. But I always felt like we were a disappointment to him. He left the raising of us to our mother. He didn't interfere. Ever. I suppose he didn't care enough to."

"So you're very cautious," he surmised.

"I am," she agreed. "I can't marry a man who wouldn't be able to love my boys with all his heart, right along with me. And that is a lot to ask. That's why I reassured the boys that I'd never marry anyone they didn't approve of. And that might have been putting too much power into young hands."

"But I understand where it's coming from now," Elias said.

"As for Liam," Delia said, "I agree that time with his grandparents will be good for him. He can help them out, learn about hard work and feeling good about pitching in. And I'm sure they'll be able to talk to him about a few things. Maybe he'll hear it differently from them."

She was a *mamm* of boys. He was a *daet* of a girl. It was different somehow. She saw a large boy in Liam. He saw a young man—one who could be a bad influence for his daughter at this stage. All the same, Liam was only visiting, and Elias would be bringing Violet back to Indiana soon enough. Young Liam was a problem for other parents.

The ride back to Swarey Flower Farm felt short with

Delia next to him. The sun was sinking low on the horizon, and the shadows stretched out long and lazy. But soon enough they'd reach home, and they'd have to face their *kinner*. He had no idea how Violet was going to react when he got back!

Elias looked over at Delia and smiled. "You're doing a good job, Delia."

And she was. Better than he was. Her *kinner* weren't questioning their faith. If Wanda had lived, she would have been able to get through to Violet—he was sure of it. Wanda and Violet had shared a special mother-daughter bond, and without Wanda, things just weren't the same. But Violet's *mamm* wasn't so easy to replace in her heart. Delia was right that it wasn't easy to find someone who could love his daughter the way he did. Was it too much to ask of a new wife? But his heart seemed to tell him that he had to ask it! Because Violet deserved to live in a home with a stepmother who loved her, and his choices would determine if she was chased out of her own home or loved as dearly as she deserved to be loved.

When they pulled into the drive, Elias spotted three of Delia's boys sitting on the front porch. They had a plate of meat and an open bag of buns. A post-dinner snack. He remembered what it felt like to be constantly hungry because he was growing. Violet sat with them— the only one on the porch swing.

Thomas sat leaning against a tree, a sandwich on the ground on a plate beside him as he slowly chewed and swallowed. He had a pair of suspenders he was working on with a needle and thread.

"Now the parenting begins," Delia murmured, and

they shared a conspiratorial laugh. She was pretty when she laughed like that, and he liked the way her brown eyes glittered. "Remember me in your prayers tonight, Elias. I might need it."

"Same here," he said. And he knew she wasn't joking when she asked for prayer. Neither was he. He reined in the horse and tied off the reins. Violet stayed on the swing, eyeing him skeptically.

Delia hopped down without help from him, and she cast him a smile as she headed over to the porch.

"Broken suspenders?" Elias asked, stopping where Thomas sat.

"Yep." The boy chewed on his lip as he tried to push the needle into the leather.

"You've got to make the holes in the leather first," Elias said. "Either that, or get one of those foot pump machines to sew it for you."

"I don't have one of those," Thomas said. "And I have to fix these."

"I have an extra pair that I could give you," Elias said.

"I don't need handouts," Thomas muttered.

Right. He wouldn't take a gift from him.

"Who's talking about handouts?" Elias said. "My buggy is really dirty, and I've got other stuff I have to do. If you wash and polish it tonight, the suspenders are yours. Fair pay for work well-done. It's up to you."

Thomas brightened but looked toward his mother warily.

"Will you tell my mother?" Thomas asked.

"That you're working for fair pay?" Elias asked. "She's paying my daughter, isn't she? I don't see a difference."

Thomas considered that for a moment, then nodded. "Okay. I'll do it."

Thomas cast him a relieved grin. The boy probably didn't have enough pocket money to buy another pair of suspenders, and he didn't want to tell his mother. Elias understood that feeling when a boy's manly instincts were starting to kick in, and he wasn't actually grown enough to take care of himself. It was a difficult time for a boy's pride, and mothers didn't always recognize it.

"Come over after I've got my buggy back over there. I'll leave it by the pump. Bring your own bucket and cloth, if you could, but we've got the soap."

"*Yah*, I can do that."

This was a point in his favor with Thomas... Now, to start doing that with the other three boys. Delia really did have her work cut out for her if she wanted these boys to accept a suitor. But she was worth it—and any man who took some time to get to know both her and the boys would see that.

He headed over to the porch, and Violet stopped swinging.

"Did you have a nice time?" Elias asked his daughter.

"It was okay," she said. "You took long enough."

"It wasn't more than two hours," he replied.

"Still."

He met Violet's petulant gaze, and she asked, "Can I go to the youth event Monday night?"

"What youth event?" he asked, and he glanced over at Delia.

"Oh, it's at the Lapp farm," Delia said as her shoes hit gravel and she straightened her skirt. "They're having volleyball and a hymn sing. My boys are going."

"They said I can go with them, if I want," Violet said, and she dug into the gravel with the toe of her shoe. "It sounded fun. I thought it might be nice to play volleyball again. I'm pretty good at it."

She was very good at volleyball, actually. She had a very good spike where she could smash the ball down over the net.

"Ezekiel will be driving them in his buggy," Delia said. "He'll be driving Beulah, his girlfriend, as well. So Violet wouldn't be the only girl in the buggy, if that concerns you."

A youth group night of fun with other Amish *kinner*. It wasn't a bad idea.

"Well, I suppose you can go," Elias said.

A smile broke over his daughter's face, and suddenly, he wasn't looking into the face of his rebellious teen anymore. This was the smile of his little girl—still under the teenager surface—and he was so glad to see that open, happy smile that a lump rose in his throat.

"*Danke*, Daet!"

"Maybe while they're all out having fun, we can have pie together," Delia said quietly. "It would be…expected, don't you think?"

A pie baked by Delia Swarey? He wouldn't turn that down! It was the time with her that piqued his interest.

"I'd be happy to come have dessert with you," he said, and he felt his own open, happy smile come to his lips. "We can compare notes over how we handled things tonight."

She tapped the side of her nose and then headed up to the front door.

Elias glanced back at Thomas. The boy was watching him.

"Delia?" Elias called after her.

*"Yah?"* She turned, and his heart took a tumble—she looked so pretty there at her own front door.

"I asked Thomas to wash my buggy tonight. Do you mind?"

Delia looked past him toward her son, then shrugged. "Not at all. He's a hard worker. He'll do a good job."

"See you later, then," he said.

And Delia smiled again, then disappeared inside.

"Let's get back," he said to Violet.

He'd explain later why he'd asked Thomas to wash his buggy, but now was not the time. And that youth event might be good for Violet, too. Violet would get a little bit of safe freedom, and Elias could get a little more advice and moral support from Delia, who was quickly becoming the answer to his own prayers.

## Chapter Five

Delia looked out the door once more as Elias and Violet hopped up into the buggy. Elias waited until his daughter was seated, and then he hoisted himself up. He was protective of Violet, and she liked to see it. Her stepfather hadn't been anything like that with her, and she couldn't help but wonder what it would have felt like to have a father taking such good care of her when she was at that age.

She turned from the window and found her boys all looking at her pointedly. Except for Thomas. He had a broken pair of suspenders in one hand and one of her good sewing needles and thread.

"Thomas, that needle with break on leather," she said.

"Sorry." He put the needle and thread onto the table, the suspenders still clutched in one fist.

"That was Aaron's fault," Moses said. "They were fighting."

"Fighting about what?" Delia demanded.

"Nothing," Thomas muttered. "It's fine."

"It's not fine if your suspenders are broken," she sighed. She'd have to get to town and get him another pair. She'd squeeze it into the grocery budget somehow.

"What did you do on your buggy ride?" Moses demanded, not to be sidelined by a pair of suspenders.

"I chatted with Elias," Delia replied. "And we stopped to bring flowers to Willa Speicher."

"I don't like it," Aaron muttered.

"I know none of you like it," she replied. "But I told you when I left that when I got back we would talk this through. And I mean for us to do just that."

"You don't even care that we don't like it!" Aaron said. "You used to say that our opinion mattered, but it doesn't seem to this time!"

Delia rubbed her hands over her face. "Sit down, boys."

"I don't want—" Aaron started.

"I said sit down!" she snapped. "Now!"

The boys plunked down into kitchen chairs, staring sullenly at the tabletop. Thomas stayed standing, leaning against the back of one kitchen chair, and she gave him a pointed look. He pulled the chair out and sat down, too.

"First of all, I am your mother," Delia said sternly. "I run this home, and I make the decisions. You are my *kinner*. That means you are to show more respect than that!"

There were some murmured apologies.

"Good." She pulled a chair out and sat down. "Now, we need to talk. I know you boys are upset, and I want you to really think about why."

"Because we don't like him," Thomas muttered.

"And why not?" she asked. "What about Elias specifically is worrisome?"

"He just wants our farm," Aaron said.

"And what makes you believe that?" she asked. "He's not asked me anything about the farm. Not how many acres we've got. Not how much we make off of flower deliveries. Nothing."

"Maybe he's asked around," Ezekiel said quietly. "He might already know more than you think."

"Have you heard any rumors of that?" she asked.

Ezekiel dropped his gaze. But she doubted they had.

"You're scared," Delia said. "I can see it in your faces, and I can tell by the way you're all reacting. You're afraid, and I want you dig down deep and figure out exactly what you're scared is going to happen. When you imagine a new *daet* in this home, what do you imagine happening?"

The boys were silent. If they'd been girls, they would have been able to tell her exactly what they were afraid of, but boys were different. They didn't like to talk about their feelings, and from what she could tell, they didn't like to look at them directly, either.

"Are you afraid he'll be harsh with you with punishments?" she asked.

"*Yah*, that would be terrible," Moses said. "He might beat us."

"He won't beat you."

"He might!" Moses said.

"Moses, do you think I would marry a man who would beat my *kinner*?" she asked gently. "Before a woman accepts a proposal, she knows exactly what the man's character is like. I would never risk something like that."

"Oh…" Moses murmured.

"Is there anything else that worries you?" Delia looked around the table. For a few beats, there was silence from them, then Aaron shifted in his seat.

"What if he sells the farm?" Aaron asked.

Good, they were starting to talk. She suppressed a smile. "Son, this farm is going to you boys. I'm not selling it."

"But he might!" Tears misted Aaron's eyes and he blinked angrily, looking away.

"And he might be lying to you when he says he won't sell it," Thomas added. "Men do that sometimes. Sometimes they're nice to someone to get them to trust them, and then whammo."

"Not good men," she replied.

"He might not be good!" Aaron chewed on the side of his cheek.

"That is why we ask around about people," she said. "That's why you find out what his community says about him, and what his family says about him. You look at his parents and his brothers and sisters and see what character they have, and you talk to elders in his community and see what they say. An Amish community helps protect us against a mistake like that because people talk."

"We don't think you should risk it," Moses said.

Delia looked over at Ezekiel. He sat with his lips pressed into a tight line. He wasn't looking at his brothers, but he did fiddle with the handle of a stray fork.

"Ezekiel?" she prompted. "What is it that scares you?"

Her eldest son's soulful gaze moved up to meet hers. "I'm not scared of him beating us or selling our farm. Maybe he won't do those things, and if he tried, I'm old enough to do something about it. He wouldn't be lifting a hand against us, I'll tell you that plainly. What scares me is if he hurts you, Mamm. I'm scared he'll break your heart or disappoint you."

Tears welled in Delia's eyes. "Oh, Ezekiel…"

"That would be the worst," Aaron whispered.

"I'd kick him in the leg, Mamm!" Moses said. "I'd do it! I would!"

It was obviously the worst thing that Moses could think of doing to retaliate and protect his *mamm*.

"No one needs to kick anyone, Moses," Delia said. "And we are Christians. We don't get revenge."

But her heart filled to overflowing for these dear boys who worried most about her getting hurt.

"Here's the truth of it," Delia said, putting a hand over Ezekiel's for a moment. "Opening your heart up to romance risks pain. I opened my heart to your father, and my heart broke when he died. That was a risk I took, and your *daet* was worth the pain. It's true that every romantic hope risks some pain, but I know one thing—" she looked around the table at her boys "—even if my heart gets broken, I have four magnificent boys who will cheer me right back up."

They looked at her somberly, and she sobered, too.

"I mean that," she said quietly. "You'll all grow up and risk a bit of heartbreak yourselves. And when you face hard times, you'll come home to me and to each other, and we'll support you. I promise to be cautious, but you can't wrap me in cotton, boys. Maybe I'll shed a tear or two, but I'll survive it."

Ezekiel's expression hardened, and Moses shook his head.

"If you cry, Mamm, I'm kicking him in the leg! I told you!" Moses said.

"Hey." Ezekiel's tone was firm. "Don't talk like that, Moses. If Mamm cries, *I'll* deal with him, myself. You won't have to worry about it."

Moses sighed and sank lower in his chair. Aaron and Thomas stared at the tabletop. And that might be as good as it was going to get tonight.

"I'd better go on over and wash that buggy," Thomas said quietly.

"Why are you doing it?" Moses demanded. "Let him wash his own buggy!"

"Moses!" Delia said.

"Moses is right," Aaron said. "You don't have to help him."

"Because...he'll give me new suspenders if I do," Thomas retorted, and he shoved his chair back with a noisy scrape. "And you're the one who broke mine, Aaron, so leave me alone! I've got to do what I've got to do."

Thomas stomped over to a cupboard and tugged out a bucket and a rag as his brothers watched him in surprise. All this for suspenders? Ezekiel was the next one to stand up, and he headed for the stairs, looking annoyed. Elias had offered exactly what Thomas wouldn't be able to refuse...

Thomas disappeared out the side door and Delia sighed. She wanted the boys to change their attitude, but she didn't want their brotherly bond broken, either. She was proud of how well her boys took care of each other, and while she needed them to back off when it came to her romantic possibilities, she didn't want them to back away from each other.

Hopefully she wasn't making a monumental mistake.

Monday evening after dinner, the boys got ready for the youth group volleyball night at the Lapp farm. Ezekiel was hogging the bathroom, and Thomas and Aaron kept pounding on the door to be let in to brush their teeth. Moses sat at the kitchen table, his shoes on his feet, ready to leave.

Delia carefully lifted an apple pie out of the oven and put it on a rack on the stovetop. Then she closed the flue.

"Can I have a piece?" Moses asked.

"Not now. It's piping hot," she replied. "When you get back tonight."

"I'll just blow on it," Moses replied.

"You're being brave but unwise." Delia chuckled. "When you get back is soon enough." She looked up the stairs. "Ezekiel, let your brothers in!"

She heard the bathroom door unlock and Aaron's and Thomas's voices mingled in complaint.

"What'll you do while we're gone?" Moses asked.

"Elias is going to come have a piece of pie with me," she said.

"What?" Moses frowned. "He's coming over when we're gone?"

"*Yah.* We've talked about this, son. It's going to be fine."

"Well…" Moses looked down. "I think my tummy is starting to hurt. I better stay home."

"Hogwash," she replied. "You'll feel fine by the time you get to youth group."

"I don't think I will." Moses rubbed his hand over his belly. "It's a sore stomach, Mamm. An awfully sore stomach. A stomach so sore, I wouldn't even eat pie."

"It only started when you heard that Elias was coming for pie," she said, bending down to his level. "That's not a tummy ache from sickness. That is a tummy ache from worry. And there is nothing to worry over, son. You need to go to youth group."

The older boys came clomping down the stairs, and Ezekiel disappeared back into the bathroom again.

"Oh, for crying out loud, Ezekiel!" Aaron hollered back up the stairs. "We'll be late! We've got to go!"

"He's trying to look perfect for Beulah," Thomas sang out, and even Moses laughed at that.

"He doesn't want to smell like a barn!" Aaron called out.

"Oh, stop it, you two," Delia said, smiling. "Go hitch up the buggy. I'm sure Ezekiel will be out soon. You don't want to be late." She gave Moses a serious look. "You, too. Off you go."

There was a knock on the side door as the boys got their shoes on. It took a busy minute with the boys slamming their feet into running shoes before they negotiated the door—the boys going outside and Elias coming in.

Moses scowled at Elias, but he followed his brothers outside with a muttered, "Hi, Violet... Come on. Ezekiel's taking forever in the bathroom."

Elias looked out the window after the boys, watching them for a moment before he turned back to the kitchen.

"She'll be fine with them," Delia said.

He smiled sheepishly. "Sometimes I worry."

Ezekiel came down the stairs then, and his gaze landed on Elias with a look of surprise.

"Right," the teenager said, glancing toward Delia.

"Have a nice night, Ezekiel," Delia said firmly. "Say hello to Beulah for me."

"I will," Ezekiel said, and he pressed his lips together. At least he wasn't going to argue about it in front of Elias, and for that Delia was thankful. "We'll see you later on."

"Be home by eleven," Delia reminded him.

"I know. 'Bye, Mamm." He didn't include Elias in his farewell as he headed out the side door. When Delia went to the window, she could see Aaron and Thomas almost finished hitching up the buggy, and Violet and Moses standing nearby watching them. Violet turned when Ezekiel came outside, and they exchanged a few words.

"That was nice of you to pay Thomas with suspenders," Delia said, turning back to the kitchen again.

"Oh...it was nothing. I just saw that he was worried about fixing his, and I figured I had a solution," Elias said.

"At least you made sure he worked for it," Delia said.

"He wouldn't have accepted them otherwise," he replied. "It's okay. I understand how boys think. A very long time ago, I was a boy that age."

Delia smiled ruefully. "Not that long, Elias. We're almost the same age. I'm forty-one and you're..."

"Forty-four. And you're right."

"Thomas worries about money sometimes," Delia said. "He shouldn't. I would have gotten him new suspenders. But they try to take on the adult worries around the farm, no matter how hard I try to stop them."

Delia headed for the kitchen and pulled down a couple of plates. "So how did it go with Violet last night?"

"Well..." Elias was silent a moment. "She's being obstinately silent about it. How about you?"

"Mine are afraid of a few things. One, that you might be harsh and beat them. Two, that you might be after the farm and not my heart. And three, that you might be a liar and break my heart."

Elias looked up at her, eyebrows raised. "Oh, wow. So that's what's worrying them. That's really something that you were able to get all of that out of them."

"I'm not sure how I did it, either," she said, depositing the plates on the table.

"So they're really worried about getting beaten?" he asked.

She glanced over her shoulder. "Zeke and I were never the harsh punishment type of people. We did more long lectures or taking away something they liked or giving extra chores to keep those idle hands busy."

"Wise parenting," Elias said quietly.

"Are you the same?" she asked. And somehow, his answer mattered—even though it shouldn't. *It didn't!* This pretend courtship was not in any permanent way between them. But she stilled to hear what he'd say, all the same.

"*Yah*, my *daet* was a harsh disciplinarian, and I don't think it did us much good. It made us angry, mostly. It didn't change our hearts. We have a much different relationship now, but when I was young, I feared him more than I loved him. I don't want that with my daughter."

"What do you do to keep Violet on the right path?" she asked.

"Maybe not enough considering her current struggles," he admitted. "But I talk to her about consequences that happen in real life. Like, the kind of world that is out there waiting for sweet Amish girls, and the kinds of people who might take advantage."

That was a good answer that even her stubborn boys would have to appreciate. She passed her hand over the

V she'd cut in the top of the pie crust. It was no longer steaming, but it still felt very hot.

"I think that's all you can do, really," Delia said. "Especially at this age. Besides extra chores, perhaps, or grounding her."

"But when the reason why she's leaning toward an Englisher life is her grief over losing her *mamm*, I'm not sure punishment is the way."

Delia nodded. "I agree. It's complicated, isn't it? We don't want to break their spirits or chase them out. We want to guide them in safe paths...and they want adventure."

She turned to reach for a knife, and somehow, her other hand connected with the hot glass pie plate. It all happened so quickly that she wasn't sure exactly how she'd done it. She let out a cry and the knife clattered to the floor.

She shook her hand, trying to cool it, and she shut her eyes against the burn.

"Delia!"

When she opened her eyes, Elias was at her side.

Elias bent down to pick up the knife and laid it on the counter, then put a hand over Delia's. She was hurt—he'd seen her hand touch the hot pie plate and the red welt that sprang up. He had crossed the kitchen to reach her without a second thought. Delia pulled her hand out of his and looked down at the burn. She grimaced.

"Ouch," she said.

"Come here." He went over to the sink and turned on the cold water, then beckoned her over. He took her wrist and plunged her hand under the cold flow. He could feel her pulse fluttering in her wrist under his fingers, and her breath came quick and shallow.

"Better?" he asked.

"Getting there…"

Holding her wrist the way he was, he was right next to her, and while he knew she was quite capable of holding her hand under water without his assistance, he found he didn't want to move. Somehow, he felt like he was helping. A little ridiculous, he knew, but not enough to make him move first.

"That was silly of me," she said, her face turned away from him. "I'm not usually that scatterbrained."

"Looks like it hurts," he murmured.

*"Yah…"* Her voice was soft.

For a moment they stood together, Delia close enough that her shoulder pressed into his chest. She was the perfect height for him, he realized—and she smelled good, like cinnamon from her baking. Not that he should be thinking these things… But she was lovely—her eyes looked like they were always ready to smile, although now she was wincing against the pain. Her hair was thick and filled up her *kapp* to the brim with her bun. He liked that, especially…

Delia pulled her hand out of the water and took a step away from him. He found himself disappointed that the moment was over, but he released her immediately. The angry red welt on her hand would need some attention. They both looked down at it.

"That's going to be painful," he said.

*"Yah.* I know. These things happen," she replied. She cast him a sidelong look. "I suppose it's been a while since I've baked a pie for a man."

Wait—that had been for him?

"You mean you made it for me…especially?" he asked.

*"Yah."* She looked up at him then, her gaze completely guileless, and he felt a rush of tenderness toward her. She'd baked for him. It wasn't like other women hadn't brought him baked goods after his wife passed away, but somehow Delia's pie felt special.

"Well…*danke*," he said. "But you don't really have to impress me, do you?"

"Maybe I'm practicing on you a little bit, too." A smile tickled her lips. "You know, for when it's the real thing and I have to show a suitor what I bring to the table. I'm not exactly known for my wonderful baking, I'm afraid."

Elias chuckled. He was doing the same thing—he couldn't help it. Under different circumstances, Delia would be a lovely woman to get to know. If his daughter were ready for that kind of step—and right now Violet wasn't.

"You bring plenty to the table, Delia," he said, taking another step back.

"Being single is challenging," she said. "It's been twenty years since I was last dating. And back then, I was a sweet young thing with a trim little waist and her whole life ahead of her. It's different now."

He remembered her from those years. She'd been pretty and sweet, and she'd had a gaggle of girlfriends she went everywhere with. He remembered Zeke pining after her from afar before he finally got up the nerve to ask her home from singing. That was how most couples got together if they met during their youth group years. It had been the same for Elias and Wanda.

"I knew you back then," Elias said. "And you're even more beautiful now."

Delia blinked at him, and color touched her cheeks. Had he said too much? Probably. He dropped his gaze. But she *was* more beautiful. Age had given her more depth in those dark eyes, more wisdom and a knowing way of meeting his gaze that made him talk when he knew he'd be wiser to keep his mouth shut. Even the faint lines in her face and around her eyes betrayed years of more smiles than frowns. But it was more than that. Her face and figure had matured into the kind of lasting beauty that would change forms over the years, but would never fade.

"Well, I now have four boys, all the worries that come with them and limited time to keep up my own home. That's a little harder to match now," she said.

He had a teenage daughter who was a bit of a challenge.

"*Yah*, I know," he said. "My daughter makes a match a little more complicated, too. Not many women see an angry teenage girl and think they'd like to help in raising her."

Delia laughed sympathetically. "If only our *kinner* appreciated how much we prioritize them."

Delia spun around, then pulled open a drawer. Inside he spotted some first aid supplies. She took out a tube of medication.

"Burn cream," she explained. "This isn't the first time I've burned myself on a pie plate."

While Delia applied cream to her hand, Elias washed

the knife in the sink, grabbed a dish towel to protect his own hand and headed over to the pie on the top of the stove.

It smelled delicious—the tang of apples and light scent of cinnamon. Gooey pie filling bubbled up as he sliced into the flaky crust. He dished up a piece onto a plate.

"I can't make you do that," Delia said.

"You aren't making me do anything," he replied. "I've been married before, remember? I know how a kitchen works."

She chuckled. "That's true."

"Before a man gets married, he's led to believe that he'll be waited on hand and foot by an adoring and beautiful woman," he said. "I mean, it's a nice fantasy for some, but it's not realistic. Marriage isn't about being waited on, or having a woman to take care of the house chores. It's a partnership—two people who love each other and pull together to build a life. And sometimes when the wife isn't feeling well, a man is in the kitchen cooking for the family. Sometimes when a husband is sick, his wife is outside mucking out stalls."

"That's the honest truth," Delia replied. "I've done the outdoor work by myself more than once when the boys were little and Zeke was sick."

"See?" Elias shot her a smile, dished up a second piece of pie and then carried the plates to the table. "I think the way your boys help out in the house is excellent preparation for real married life."

"That's a relief, because I feel like I'm failing half the time. I can't be both a *mamm* and a *daet*. And I can't keep up with all the work by myself, either. It's been hard. But I can't get married just to get help around here, either, can I?"

"Can't you?"

Their gazes met, and he saw her consider for a moment.

"No," she said. "I can't."

"The boys?" he asked.

"My heart!" Her gaze flashed fire. "Marriage is wonderful, but it's hard work, too. I can't imagine sharing so much with someone I didn't love. Until I find a man I can truly love and trust with my boys, I'm not taking those vows again. When I was young, it was only my heart at stake. Now, it's my boys' hearts, too. I can manage."

He waited until she took her seat, and then he sat, too.

"I didn't mean to be flippant," he said. "I do agree. I mean, I've had plenty of women introduced to me in hopes that I'd choose one, but…I couldn't do it."

"Is it hard to think of being married to someone other than your late wife?" she asked gently.

"A little."

"It's the same for me… It's hard to imagine it." She nodded. "But with time, it's getting easier to start thinking about marriage again. But finding a man whom the boys will love, too…that's the hard part!"

"Delia, you can afford to be picky," he said earnestly. "I mean that. Don't worry."

In fact, he liked the idea of her waiting—not wasting herself on some man who'd gladly take over her farm. She was a woman who deserved the best, and somehow he'd feel better if she held out for just that.

"And by the way, this pie looks amazing," he added.

Delia shot him a smile. "*Danke*. I did try—both with raising my boys and baking the pie."

Elias laughed at her little joke, and Delia passed him a fork. He let his fingers linger over hers as he accepted the utensil.

"Are you really practicing on me?" she asked.

"Why? What am I doing wrong?" he asked.

"Nothing. You're just...you're a very sweet man, Elias. I don't think you need practice at all. You're charming."

He felt some heat hit his own face then. She thought he was charming, did she? Hopefully that wouldn't change! He turned his attention to the pie. They each took a bite, and for the next couple of minutes, Elias simply enjoyed the dessert. Flaky crust, sweet, tangy center, and tender apple slices.

"Do you think you could talk with Violet about...the Amish life, and the safety of staying here?" he asked. "She's heard it all from me, but I have a feeling it will be different coming from you."

"I'll get her to help me do dishes in the morning," Delia said. "I have a good excuse." She held up her burned hand.

"Even I'd help you with dishes," he said with a low laugh.

"That won't give me time alone with Violet, though," she said. "Leave it to me and Violet. Two women doing dishes get to talking. It's just the way of things."

Of all the women to help him and Violet through this difficult stage of getting used to the idea of romance again, Delia was absolutely perfect. She was kind and understanding, and he had a feeling that Violet's young heart was perfectly safe in her keeping.

## Chapter Six

It was after ten when the buggy came rattling up the drive, and the sound of boys' laughter filtered through the night air and into the cozy kitchen where Delia and Elias sat with empty mugs in front of them.

Her hand hurt. The burn ached, and while she knew the burn cream would help, there would be a few painful days before it started to heal properly. She watched as Elias went to the window and shaded his eyes to look out into the darkness. She could tell the moment he spotted his daughter, because his shoulders relaxed. She stifled a smile.

This evening had been nice, even with the burn. Spending the evening with Elias—a strong, capable, gentle man—had been a treat. The other men she'd spent time with who'd been interested in courting her hadn't been half as good company. She'd felt quizzed and judged as they tried to see if she measured up to their own personal requirements. Never mind her own needs in a husband!

"This was fun," Delia agreed. "Maybe it's just easier with no pressure."

Elias seemed to understand, because he met her gaze and nodded slowly. "I think it must be."

Moses came clattering up the stairs and he opened the side door. "Hi, Mamm! We're back! I was on the team with the big kids!"

"I'd better head out," Elias said, and he shot Moses a smile. "Good for you, Moses. Did you win?"

"No, we lost," Moses said. "And we lost badly. It was probably because of me on the team, but they didn't mind very much."

"These things happen," Elias said with a chuckle. "But they obviously enjoyed your company, Moses."

"Do you think?" Moses asked.

"*Yah.* They let you play, and they didn't mind about the points. I think they definitely liked having you there. You're a likable kid."

Moses's ears grew pink, and Delia could see the battle going on inside him. Moses looked like he wasn't sure if he should allow himself to be pleased with Elias or not.

"Help your *mamm* with chores tonight, okay?" Elias added. "She's hurt her hand."

"What happened to your hand, Mamm?" Moses came over to inspect Delia's burn, and Elias met her gaze as her son looked over her hand.

"I burned it…" she said.

Elias winked at her, and it was Delia's turn to feel her face grow warm. That Elias sure had a way with him! Then he headed for the door and slipped out.

A few minutes later, the other boys came inside, and they started rummaging through the kitchen for a snack.

"How is Beulah doing, Ezekiel?" Delia asked.

"She's good." Ezekiel came up with an apple and took a crunching bite. "She was really nice to Violet…but I don't think Violet appreciated it much."

"Why not?" Delia asked.

"Because Violet spent all her time with the Englisher boy," Aaron said, pulling down a container of muffins. The boys circled around and they all took a muffin each, and peeled the paper off the bottoms.

"You mean Liam, the Speicher grandson?" Delia asked.

"*Yah*, that's him," Aaron replied. "He's visiting his grandparents and doesn't understand even simple Pennsylvania Dutch. So we had to keep everything in English for him, and Violet flirted with him shamelessly."

Delia rubbed a hand over her eyes. "Oh, dear... I didn't think of that."

"Think of what?" Thomas asked.

"It doesn't matter," she sighed. "And how did Liam respond?"

"He had a girl fawning all over him," Ezekiel said. "He liked that a lot."

"He's trouble, though," Aaron said. "I heard some of the other boys talking, and they said that he was arrested for shoplifting and he's got a record now."

"My, my..." Delia sighed. "Well, the hope was that Liam would find some positive influences with good Christian *kinner*."

The boys didn't answer—not that she really expected them to. What were they supposed to do? But Delia hadn't anticipated that Violet would be drawn to the Englisher teenager, and she should have! She was so used to raising boys that she didn't take note of the pitfalls waiting for girls anymore.

"I don't even know why she likes him so much," Moses said past a mouthful of muffin.

"Because he's Englisher," Ezekiel replied. "That makes him dangerous and interesting."

"It just means he dresses weird and isn't very good at volleyball," Moses retorted.

The boys laughed.

"No making fun of Englishers," Delia said with a frown. "I am not raising bullies."

"We were nice to him, up until he started giving Violet too much attention," Thomas said.

"What did you do?" Delia demanded.

"I told him that we were the ones bringing her home, and he'd better not get any ideas," Thomas replied.

Delia chuckled. "Violet was well protected."

"We did tell her *daet* we'd bring her home on time," Ezekiel said irritably.

"*Danke* for looking out for her, boys," Delia said. "She's been through a lot losing her *mamm*, and she thinks that life is easier out there with the Englishers. She's wrong, of course, but...she's not very old."

A girl trying to be strong...that's all Violet was, and Delia wished she could just wrap that girl in her arms and take away her heartbreak and her confusion. But she couldn't.

"Mamm burned herself," Moses announced after a beat of silence.

"How bad?" Ezekiel asked, and the attention was turned to Delia's hand, and then to the pie, and for a few minutes they were just a family enjoying each other's company. Her boys were growing up to be fine young men, and she was proud of them.

\* \* \*

The next morning when Violet arrived to start working, Delia welcomed her into the house.

"Come in, come in," Delia said. "The boys are going to get started outside, and I was hoping you could help me out with a couple of things here in the kitchen. I burned myself yesterday, so washing dishes will be hard."

"My *daet* said you hurt yourself," Violet said. "Can I see?"

The curiosity that came with injury. Delia pulled off the piece of gauze and revealed the red blistering burn. Violet winced.

"*Yah*, I'll help with dishes. That looks painful."

"It'll heal," Delia said. "But I appreciate the help."

The boys headed out to start working in the flower fields. There was a van coming to collect long-stemmed roses from the greenhouse that afternoon, so they'd have to have the stems all freshly cut and put in a water solution with sugar and citric acid mixed in to make sure the blooms would survive as long as possible.

Delia put the plug in the sink and started the dishwater. Violet took over from there.

"How was the volleyball night?" Delia asked as she wiped down a counter.

"It was fun."

"*Yah?* Do you like the *kinner* from around here?"

"*Yah.* I guess."

"Did you make any new friends?"

"*Yah*, a few."

"Did you meet Liam?"

Violet stopped in the middle of putting a plate into

the sudsy water and glanced over her shoulder at Delia. She looked wary.

"Why?" Violet asked.

"I heard you were getting to know him," Delia replied. "He's my friend Lydia's nephew. Is he nice?"

"*Yah*, he's very nice," she replied, and her cheeks reddened.

"When I was your age, there was a boy I liked a lot named Nehemiah," Delia said. "He was two years older than me, and he was so handsome. He was a flirt, though. And I thought that I was the only one he was flirting with. Then I saw him at the dry goods store, leaning on the counter and making eyes at the cashier, and...well, I learned a thing or two."

"You think Liam is a flirt?" Violet asked.

"I think he's a troubled boy, and he probably knows how to make a girl feel special," Delia replied.

"Maybe I'm troubled, too." Violet's chin came up.

"I know you've been through a lot losing your *mamm*," Delia said.

"Did my *daet* tell you that?" Violet turned back to washing dishes, her slim shoulders hunched over the job.

"I lost my husband, sweetie," Delia said quietly, picking up a dish from the drying rack. "And my boys lost their father. In one day everything turned upside down and was never the same again. I know what it's like. And I don't say that to tell you that it's nothing. It's horrible. It changes you forever. I get it!"

"I'm planning on going English, anyway," Violet said, casting her a sidelong look.

"Are you really?"

"*Yah.* So I should make a few Englisher friends, right?"

Violet wanted a reaction from her, and Delia put the dried dish on the counter thoughtfully. Her next reaction needed to be the right one, and she sent up a silent prayer.

"Your *daet*'s heart would truly break," she said finally.

"He wants me to be like him. He wants me to be Amish, and marry some boring farmer and have babies."

"It's a beautiful life," Delia murmured. "I married a farmer and had babies."

"Oh—right." The girl's cheeks blazed red. "I'm sorry."

"No, you're being honest, and I appreciate that," Delia replied. "What kind of life do you want?"

"I want… I want to live in a city and drive a car and meet a man who loves me, and…"

"And get married and have babies?" Delia finished for her.

"Maybe. Or maybe just get married and not have babies. Sometimes Englishers don't, just because. And we'd watch TV in the evenings and ride a subway and go to coffee shops and text each other on our cell phones."

"How will you pay the bills?" Delia asked. "Someone has to work and pay for the cell phones and the TV and the life in the city. It costs quite a lot."

"I'd get a job with a rich lady, and I'd help her with her shopping," Violet replied. "Or maybe I'd open a store that sells pottery that I make myself, and I'd open a shop on a busy corner. Or I could sell umbrellas—all different kinds. I'd find something I could do. And my husband and I will have a big, beautiful apartment, and each of us will have a car to drive. And we'll eat at restaurants twice a week."

Where had Violet gotten all of these ideas? It sounded like a pretty pricey lifestyle to fund with pottery and umbrellas.

"What is it about that life that sounds the most exciting to you?" Delia asked.

"I'd meet a man who wouldn't want me because I could cook his meals or sew his clothes. He'd want me because…because—" she got a wistful look on her face "—because his heart longed for mine."

"I have news for you," Delia said softly. "Amish men don't get married for a cook and a seamstress. They get married because they want love and commitment, too."

Violet shook her head. "It's not the same, though. You should hear how my grandparents talk about you."

Delia froze. They talked about her? "What do they say?"

"They say you're a middling to fair cook and a very good mother," Violet said.

Delia rolled the comments over in her mind. Well… that could have been worse. She would have preferred something a little more glowing about her cooking, but she could accept their assessment.

"I think that's a fair estimation of me," Delia admitted.

"Do you really want a man tallying up how well you cook when he decides if he wants to marry you?" Violet demanded. "Or how well you sew, or how well you knit? Do you want him to be considering how clean your kitchen is?"

That stung, because Delia's kitchen wasn't terribly clean these days. Teenagers had a way of finding an adult's sensitive spot, didn't they?

"Sweetie, regardless of what life you lead, Amish or English, people are going to judge you. If you go English, they'll have things they look at. Maybe how you dress, or how you do your hair. Here, we all dress the same, and we all do our hair the same. But out there, there will be judgment, too."

But by the set to the girl's jaw, Delia didn't think that Violet was really hearing her. She had a fantasy in her mind about an Englisher life, and she didn't want it popped. But Violet washed all the dishes, rinsed them well and left them in the dish rack for Delia to dry. She did the job well, wiped off the surrounding counter and hung up the rag.

"My *daet* wants a woman who will raise me," Violet said, turning toward Delia. "He's considering you for that job. He wants a cook, too. And a woman who will make a home comfortable. And you are getting to know him. I understand that. But I want more than that for myself, and I won't pretend otherwise."

If Delia ever did marry again, she wanted more than that, too. The girl made a good argument. Every woman wanted to be more than the jobs she did in the home. More than mother and cook and seamstress and caregiver. Every woman wanted to open up that part of a man's heart that glowed just for her.

"Can I go work in the greenhouse now?" Violet asked.

"*Yah*, go ahead. Thank you for helping me," Delia said. "This will count as your work hours, of course."

Violet nodded and headed for the door. Then she turned with her hand on the knob.

"Delia?" she said, her voice suddenly softer.

"*Yah?*"

"You don't have to pay me for dishes. That was because your hand is hurt," Violet said. "Just start paying me for the work when I get out there."

"Oh…" Delia looked at the girl in surprise. "Are you sure?"

"*Yah.* I hope your hand gets better soon," Violet said, and then she disappeared out the door.

A lump rose in Delia's throat. Just a girl trying to be strong, and deep in Violet's heart, she knew she was worth more than her housework. And she was! But how to explain to a girl that we can be worth more than our skills and our abilities, but we still need to bring those skills and abilities to the table all the same?

But Violet was afraid of the very same things that Delia was—not truly holding a man's heart. And under it all, Violet really was a sweet girl, but a sweet girl who was leaning in a very dangerous direction.

Elias spent the morning helping his parents pack, and it seemed that for everything he put into a box, his *daet* would take out two items he needed for some project or other. He refused to leave the house in bad repair for Elias's sister Mary and her husband, who'd be moving in. So half the time, Elias was helping his *daet* fix hinges or repair creaking steps or the running toilet.

And when his *daet* went to "rest his eyes" in the rocking chair, and his *mamm* disappeared into the garden to putter, Elias heaved a quiet sigh. He was happy to help his parents. It was nice to spend time with them again, but it was exhausting, too. His father was an old man now, and he acted like one. He wasn't the strong, quick-thinking head of the family anymore, and that was both the natural progression of things and sad, too. Because now, Elias was the one making the plans and organizing things. He was the one telling his *daet* when it was enough, and they had to pack those tools away. And yet, he didn't want to make his father feel bad, either, so this process had become incredibly slow, and tiring for Elias, too.

With his parents otherwise occupied, Elias decided to take a little break of his own, and he headed out across the scrub grass toward the Swarey Flower Farm. He wanted to see how his daughter was faring, and he had to admit that he was looking forward to seeing Delia, too. If the timing were different and the *kinner* were ready for a stepparent, he might be looking a little more seriously at Delia. She was…oddly comforting. It had been a long time since he'd felt anything but caution in a single woman's presence.

He passed the fields of flowers spread out in neat rows—rows of pink, white, red and purple. The scent of blooms permeated the air, and he inhaled deeply. The smell of flowers was becoming entangled in his mind with Delia these days, and he wondered if the scent of a bloom was going to bring back memories of the Swarey family when he was back home again.

He spotted Violet carrying a black bucket filled with flowers, and behind her came one of the boys—that would be Thomas—a good head and shoulders taller than Violet was. Ezekiel stood next to several buckets of blooms with a clipboard in one hand, and Delia peered around his shoulder, pointing at something on the page.

Then Delia looked up and spotted Elias. She waved, said something else to her son, who nodded, and then

Delia headed in his direction. They looked busy this morning—he didn't want to get in the way, but he was interested to hear how Delia's talk with his daughter went. He had a feeling Violet wouldn't mention it.

"Elias!" Delia said as she reached him. "How is the packing going?"

"Slowly," he replied. "You look busy here."

"We have a truck coming this afternoon to pick up a large flower shipment," she replied. "So we're getting ready for it."

"I should probably let you get back to it, then," Elias said.

"Actually, Elias—" She glanced over her shoulder toward Ezekiel and the flowers. "Do you want to walk with me just a little bit? There was something I should tell you."

"Oh." This sounded serious.

Elias fell into step beside her and they ambled across the grass and toward the drive that led up to the road. Delia walked slowly, leaving a proper eighteen inches between them.

"How did your talk with Violet go?" he asked.

"I fear that I may have caused trouble."

That didn't sound likely, but he trusted Delia's instincts, too. "How?"

"Well, I had mentioned the youth volleyball night to Willa Speicher, and they sent their grandson, Liam—the Englisher boy we saw at their place—to the youth night." She shot him a cautious look, and suddenly, he knew what was coming. A rebellious but moderately good-looking young Englisher. His daughter who wanted nothing more than to marry an Englisher and escape her Amish life...

"And Violet took a shine to him?" he asked.

"*Yah*, I'm afraid so. My boys told me about it last night, and I made sure to talk to her, myself. I told you I'd help."

"I appreciate it..." he murmured.

"She didn't tell me much about Liam," Delia went on. "I tried to give her a few things to think about, but she wouldn't admit much. It was my boys who told me that she and Liam were together most of the evening."

Elias rubbed his hands over his face. Just great! Now, his daughter had a boy, just the right age to intrigue her, but too old for her all the same, to put her attention into. That was not a reassuring thought!

"We won't be here too much longer, at least," he said finally.

"This morning she was telling me about her plans to marry an Englisher and run a pottery shop in the middle of a busy town or something like that. Girlish dreams, really. Nothing realistic."

"What does she want from that life?" he asked help-lessly. "I give her everything! I work hard to provide for her, I bring her to service, help her visit her friends and aunts and uncles... I do everything I can to make sure her life is full and content. What does she want so badly?"

"She says..." Delia licked her lips and her gaze flick-ered up toward him uncertainly. "She says she wants to be worth more than her housework. As a woman."

"Of course women are worth more than housework!" he barked out, and Delia startled. He lowered his voice—

he hadn't meant to scare her. "Sorry. But obviously, she is. Every woman is worth more than cooking and cleaning."

Delia shrugged. "I don't know what to tell you, Elias. That's her worry. That all people see is how good she can sew or bake or jar pickles. And she wants someone to see deeper—to see her as a person."

"But a woman needs to know how to keep house," Elias said.

"So does a man, at least a bit," Delia added.

"Don't I know it," he replied with a sigh. "I was cooking, cleaning and going to work all on my own after Wanda passed away."

Delia nodded. "I know. And I'm trying to keep up with everything on my own over here. It's good for a woman to know how to care for the livestock and run the farm. But I think she fears that a potential husband will judge her based on her homemaking skills, and she longs to simply be loved for who she is."

"I do love her for who she is." He felt the implied judgment there.

"Oh, I know, Elias. I can tell! And there is the fact that a woman has to bring certain skills to her marriage. In order for any young person to be ready for marriage, they have to know how to do their part of the work. A young wife and mother has to know how to cook, clean, care for *kinner*, preserve food, make clothes… Being ready for a role doesn't mean she's only valued for her skills. It just means that she's ready to step into that responsibility."

"And the same for a young man," he agreed. "He has to be able to provide for a family before he marries. It's not enough to love the girl. He'd better be able to provide for her and the *kinner* that come along. But I like how you put that. You're right. A certain set of skills is needed for a romance to survive."

"They are so eager to put the cart ahead of the horse," Delia said quietly. "But their hearts aren't ready for marriage, either. It takes time."

"I wish we lived closer to each other," Elias said softly. "You make things make sense."

Delia smiled at that. "*Danke*. I do try."

A large white delivery truck turned into the drive and came slowly toward them.

"The truck is early," Delia said, and she cast Elias a panicked look. "Would you mind lending a hand for a few minutes?"

"*Yah*, sure!"

He followed her as she gathered up her skirt and jogged ahead of the truck back toward the house. There was work to be done, and he'd be glad to help her out. This was a man's life—helping those around him, and being the strong support the women in his life needed.

If only Violet could see that his hard work, the long hours, his stubborn determination to make sure she was in new dresses and every single shopping trip to town that cost too much so that he could bring home cooking supplies…all of that equalled love.

Elias helped to hoist buckets filled with water and long-stemmed flowers up into the back of the truck, and Violet was kept busy cutting flowers in the greenhouse, far from him. Not that he could talk to her with everyone around…and he didn't have the words yet, either. He was still praying for Gott to give him some sort of wisdom, some words that would cut through that fog of hers and show her how life really was, and how beautiful their Amish world was, too.

The next couple of hours passed quickly, and he was impressed at how professional Ezekiel was through the whole process. He kept everyone on task and the flowers coming in a steady flow to be loaded up. He checked and double-checked the paperwork, had the driver sign... Ezekiel was truly a man now, it seemed, and Elias could only imagine how proud Delia must be to have raised him.

Speaking of being ready for marriage, Ezekiel was well on his way. He'd be a hardworking provider for his own family in a few years, Elias was sure.

When the truck rumbled away, Delia waved to Ezekiel, and then disappeared back into the greenhouse where Violet was working. Maybe she was going to give the girl some more advice...and he should probably leave the women alone for that. He'd asked for Delia's help, after all.

"Violet's working hard," Ezekiel said.

Elias startled, and looked toward the young man. "Good. I'm really glad."

"My *mamm* really likes her," Ezekiel said. "We're all of us men here at the farm. I think she likes having a girl around, too."

"Well, Gott gives what he gives," Elias said with a chuckle. "I know she's awfully proud of you boys."

"We almost had a sister," Ezekiel said quietly. "Mamm was getting pretty big when she lost the baby. It had been a little girl."

Elias felt those words like a punch to the gut. He had never heard about that. "What a terrible loss…"

"*Yah*. It was about three years ago. Before my *daet* died."

Elias let out a slow breath. He'd been married for nearly twenty years when his wife passed away, and Wanda had lost two pregnancies before Violet. He understood what that did to a woman. It broke her heart, gutted her. It would leave her a shell for a long time while she tried to pull herself together. It took the women in her family and in her community to get her through it.

"Your *mamm* is an extraordinary woman," he said in a quiet voice.

"She is," Ezekiel said. "And I wanted to apologize for threatening you before. We're protective of our *mamm* because she's strong and smart and wonderful, but she's vulnerable, too. We know that better than anyone. So when I said not to hurt her…I meant, please be careful with my mother's heart. She's wonderful, but she's lost a lot, too. My *daet*, our baby sister… She deserves some peace, don't you think?"

Elias met the young man's gaze, and instead of anger in those dark eyes, he saw pleading. Delia did deserve some peace. She deserved kindness and support…and not to have her heart toyed with by the likes of him. Ezekiel didn't know that their arrangement already protected his mother's heart, but it was up to Elias to check his softer feelings that had started developing toward Delia. She was a lovely woman, but her boys weren't out of control, either. They knew her life better than anyone, and they wanted to keep their mother safe from anyone who would cause her more pain.

"I understand, Ezekiel," Elias said kindly. "You're a good son. I will be very careful not to hurt her. That's a promise, man to man."

*"Danke,"* Ezekiel said.

That was a promise Elias meant to keep.

## Chapter Seven

That evening, Delia stood in the kitchen alone. The boys had gone out for pizza with some cousins, and the house felt empty. One day, her boys would grow up, and this would be her life—a silent house and a full heart. If Zeke had lived, they'd live a quiet life together. The thought put a lump in her throat. Was it wrong for a mother to wish everything could freeze at this age, and the boys would remain under her roof forever?

Maybe it was. She hung a dish towel over the oven handle.

Her boys wanted nothing more than to grow up just as fast as they could, and she remembered being the same at their age, but she'd had more pressures around her back then. She'd been in a home with a stepfather who had been disinterested at best. Joseph had loved their mother, but she couldn't say he'd loved his stepchildren. Not truly. He'd provided for them. He'd given advice if they wanted to hear it. And he'd stepped back and let Mamm do the rest. He'd raised them, not loved them. There was a difference. It was that difference that was scaring Violet so much, and truthfully, it was a daunting thought for Delia, too.

So Delia had longed for her own home and family from then on. She'd wanted to move out of her mother's home and find a place where she could be the heart and center. Her boys already were the beating heart of this home, and she never let them forget it. And yet, they still yearned to grow up so much faster than Delia was ready for. As a *mamm*, she no longer felt like she was leading these boys. She was jogging behind them!

Outside she heard the clop of hooves. The boys wouldn't be back already, would they? She headed over to the window to look out at a buggy making its way toward the house, and she recognized her stepfather's grizzled face.

Joseph? What was he doing here?

She'd long since stopped trying to call the man Daet. They'd agreed together that she could simply call him by his first name after she got married. It was more comfortable for both of them.

Joseph reined in the horse, and for a moment he just sat unmoving, his shoulders slumped. Then he seemed to rouse himself, and he slowly descended from the buggy. He had a little paper bag in one hand that he carried almost gingerly. Her stepfather had never, in all her adult years, come to visit her. Not alone. He'd come with her mother and would sit quietly with a cup of coffee while her mother would do the visiting for both of them.

But Joseph never came alone. Delia's heartbeat sped up. Was it bad news?

Her mother, Linda, had come to visit just the week before and had told her that she thought Joseph was getting more difficult as he got older. He was pickier and being critical. Linda didn't like to complain, and she hadn't given any details, but Delia couldn't help but wonder what would bring her stepfather over.

She headed for the door and opened it, waiting while Joseph put a bucket of water and some feed within the horse's reach. He paused with a hand on the animal's neck, then he turned toward the house and gave Delia a somber look.

"Joseph?" she said. "Is everything all right?"

He didn't answer, but he did cock his head to one side. "For the moment, I suppose it is. But I think we should talk."

Joseph stopped at the steps, and he looked at her uncertainly. Joseph had never seemed terribly comfortable around Delia. He'd become her stepfather when she was fourteen, and that might have something to do with it. Fourteen-year-old girls could be terrifying in their own right. But Delia was well past the age of teenage angst.

"Is Mamm all right?" she asked.

"Can I come in, Delia?" he asked gently. That wasn't an answer.

"Of course." She stood back, and Joseph plodded up the steps, the little paper bag held in front of him as if it contained a snake. He stepped out of his boots, then handed the bag over to her.

"For me?" she asked.

"Sort of. Your mother made those cookies."

She looked inside the bag to see two big chocolate chip cookies. Her mother was an excellent baker, and she smiled. It was just like Mamm to send along a little gift, although she still wondered why her mother hadn't come along for this visit.

"*Danke*, Joseph."

Joseph just eyed her.

"Take a bite," he said.

"Now? I thought I'd save them for—" But there was something in his expression that made her stop. "What's going on?"

"Just…taste it," he said.

Delia reached in for a cookie and took one small bite, and the overwhelming taste of salt touched her tongue. She immediately spit the bite of cookie back into the bag.

"Oh!" she gasped.

"It's not the first time. Or the second, either," Joseph said. "This is about the fifth time she's mixed up the salt and sugar."

Her mother had said that her husband was getting critical…but this did seem odd.

"Is it the containers?"

"No, the salt is in a box of table salt. The sugar is in a bag of sugar." He pulled out a kitchen chair and sat down. "I'm not here to complain about your *mamm*'s cooking, Delia. I'm here to tell you that I think something's very wrong."

And Joseph began to talk about his life with Linda. He told Delia about how she'd started to forget to start supper, and how she'd been stumped when it came to tallying up a row of numbers—something she'd always been very good at. She'd claimed she was tired, and she had every right to be! Some days were better and she was the same old Linda, and her mind was sharp, but other days she'd started mixing up ingredients when she cooked—badly mixing up ingredients. She'd made bread without yeast and rhubarb pie without sugar. She'd bought five large bags of flour—one after another—

because she forgot she had flour at home. She'd taken money out of the bank account and forgotten why. He'd found a stash of bills inside the cutlery drawer after a check bounced.

"But I saw her last week," Delia said. "And she seemed...fine! She came by for tea."

Linda had seemed like her normal self, but she'd been openly irritated with Joseph, and it wasn't like an Amish woman to complain about her husband. It wasn't done.

"I know," Joseph said. "That was a good day. Like I said, not all of her days are bad ones. But the bad ones are getting more plentiful."

"What could be happening?" Delia asked.

"I don't know. I don't want to talk to anyone else, because it would hurt her feelings to know I talked about her private weaknesses behind her back. So I came to you. She can't be angry if I only talked to you, can she?"

And he honestly seemed to be asking if she could indeed be mad at him. Her heart went out to the older man.

"She should see a doctor," Delia said. That was the only answer.

"I agree. But she won't go."

"Won't?" Delia shook her head. "Why?"

"She says she's fine. She doesn't think she's all that forgetful, and she gets angry at me when I suggest it. It's become a point of contention between us, and I've prided myself on never causing your *mamm* a day of grief, but she's been angry with me a lot lately."

"*Yah...*" She knew that to be true.

"I think you should know that I'm not being difficult with her. I don't know what she's told you. I'm taking care of the chores, and I'm not complaining when the food is wrong. But once last week she left the chicken out overnight and she was furious with me for not eating it. We had to throw it out…we'd have gotten food poisoning otherwise, but she didn't remember leaving it out, you see. And I can't always just keep her happy."

"No, of course not, Joseph. I didn't know this was happening! If I'd known…"

But if Delia had known, then what? She was running a flower farm, raising four boys on her own and keeping everything running. The thought of one more problem on her plate made her want to sit down and just cry. Joseph seemed to see the look on her face, because he cleared his throat uncomfortably and shifted in his seat.

"I don't mean to be any trouble to you, either, Delia," Joseph said.

"I know, Joseph. It's okay. I think the most important thing is to get my mother to see a doctor."

"How?" he asked.

"Well…" Delia sighed. "I'll tell you what. You make an appointment for her to see a doctor, and I'll come over and talk her into going to it."

*"Danke,"* he said. "I appreciate that. She thinks it's me who's changing, you see. She thinks I'm the problem."

"We'll do our best," Delia said. "We'll start there. If she won't listen to me, then we'll bring Aunt Agnes."

Aunt Agnes was Linda's younger sister. And if Agnes couldn't do it, then they'd have to involve the church elders. She'd have to listen to them!

Delia's mind was ticking forward to future solutions, but the one thing she was dreading most was sitting down with her own mother and telling her that she needed help. Linda had always been a strong woman. She'd been the one who held up everyone else single-handedly! She'd been the one to hold Delia while she cried over the loss of her baby girl. She'd been the one to step in and help cook and clean when Zeke died. She'd ordered around a whole army of Amish ladies who'd come to help. Mamm was all heart and determination. She was a pillar of the family, and she wouldn't take kindly to being told she was slipping.

Joseph pushed himself to his feet.

"I'd best be going," he said.

Delia looked down at the salt-heavy cookies. "Joseph, are you hungry?"

"I wouldn't turn down a sandwich," he said hopefully.

Delia smiled and turned toward the kitchen. She'd put together something hearty for him.

"Where is Mamm now?" Delia asked.

"She's at home," he said. "She's drying her hair."

Mamm had long white hair, and on hair-washing night, she'd sit in the kitchen with a comb as she combed out her long hair and let it dry.

"Well, I'll make you a sandwich, and then I'll see her right away," Delia said. "And I'll talk to her."

"*Danke*, Delia. I truly appreciate it."

After eating a thick chicken sandwich, Joseph took his hat off the peg on the wall and replaced it on his head. "*Danke* again, Delia."

As her stepfather headed back out to his buggy, Delia went to the window and watched him as he crossed the gravel and heaved himself back up into the seat. Was it just her, or did the older man seem to be walking a little bit lighter now?

Delia exhaled a shaky sigh.

*Oh, Gott*, she prayed. *Whatever do I do about my mother?*

It seemed that Delia was now at the stage of life when she was the one to provide solutions—for her children, for Violet, for her stepfather, for her mother… Suddenly, when Delia hadn't been looking, she'd become the sole adult expected to fix things.

And for one fleeting moment, she wished she could go back in time to when someone else had all the answers!

Elias stood in the stable brushing down the big standardbred horse using strong, long strokes. The gelding quivered with pleasure as Elias worked. His *daet* still brushed down the horse, but it took a little more muscle to do a really thorough job of it. He'd asked his daughter to come out to help him in the barn, not because he needed the help, but because he wanted an opportunity to talk to her alone.

Violet leaned against a rail, chewing one side of her cheek. Today, she looked like thirteen going on twenty-five.

"So who told you?" she demanded. "Was it Delia?"

Violet would love to have someone to blame this on—someone other than herself. But Violet had been the one carrying on with an Englisher boy, and that was bound to draw attention. It was also a problem, and she knew it.

"I heard from two different sources this afternoon," Elias replied. "One of which was your grandmother, and she heard from no less than three others! People talk, Violet."

Violet looked away, and she scuffed the toe of her running shoe across the cement floor.

"I just wanted to…ask you about it," Elias said, keeping his voice gentle as he continued to brush the horse.

Violet didn't answer.

"Maybe you didn't know that the boy was flirting with you—or that he looked like he was," Elias suggested.

"I knew he liked me. And why shouldn't he?" she said. "We didn't do anything wrong. We just talked."

"Okay…" Elias stopped his brushing and moved around the horse to the other side. "But he's a born and raised Englisher. I know you are intrigued by their world, but those boys are raised differently. They might… expect…different things."

"He's got Amish grandparents and extended family," she replied, her tone very sure.

Elias looked at his daughter, and she met his gaze defiantly. Was she just trying to get a rise out of him? She didn't know the world like he did, and he didn't want her to. But maybe it was time to wise her up a little bit.

"Let's say that you and Liam were both older," he said. "Let's say that you were old enough to consider marriage."

Violet went still, but her angry gaze softened. She seemed to like that idea.

"Let's imagine that you were at the point of making a choice—stay Amish or go English," he went on. "And you wanted to go English. You've told me that repeatedly. Let's say Liam wants you to go English, too. He wants you to be together."

Violet licked her lips. "I would go before I was baptized so I couldn't be shunned," she said. "I've thought of that."

"All right," Elias said, nodding. "Let's say you've done that. But you move to the city, and I'm on the acreage. You run out of money. You're working really hard at a job as a waitress and even with good tips, you're struggling to make ends meet. Things have gone wrong—let's say you had a roommate, but she left and you're responsible for all the rent alone. What then?"

"If…the man loved me, he'd marry me," she said. "And then I wouldn't struggle anymore."

"But what if he didn't want to get married?" Elias asked.

"He would."

"Ah, but he wasn't raised Amish, my dear girl. So let's say he's not ready to get married. He wants to wait a while longer—have more money, and be more sure. What then?"

"Then…I keep working hard," she said.

"But the bills keep piling up," he said.

"I could ask you for help," she said.

"And I would give you help—I'd let you come live with me at home again. But I wouldn't have money to send you each month, so you'd have to come home."

"I wouldn't. I'd work it out!" she said.

And that was his fear—that even if she needed his help, she wouldn't come back. He'd have lost his daughter to the world beyond the fence.

"What if this boy…Liam, maybe…had a solution. What if he asked you to be his roommate? You could live with him. As his girlfriend," Elias said.

Violet's cheeks pinked. "But…"

"And it would solve the money issues," he added. "And maybe you'd get married later. Lots of people do it. Not Amish people, but people."

Violet was silent. She would never admit to even considering such a thing, but he knew that life out there could be very hard. And sometimes people considered options they never thought they would. And since she wasn't immediately saying she wouldn't, he could see her considering what that would be like.

"But after you moved in," Elias went on, "and you were cooking for him and cleaning for him and being just like his wife, let's say he still doesn't feel ready for marriage. What then? Then your heart is on the line. And breaking up would mean finding somewhere else to live. It would mean facing hardship alone again. It would mean losing the man you loved."

Violet pressed her lips together, and he could see her thinking hard.

"But what if he would marry me?" she asked at last.

"And what if he didn't? I've heard of it happening a few times, actually. Those are the stories I hear from adults when the *kinner* are at youth group."

Violet fell silent again.

"That's the problem. If marriage matters to you because you were raised Amish, but not to him, that's a big hurdle in a relationship. A lot of times men don't want to give the commitment and the vows. They don't want to take responsibility for a wife and *kinner*. They see a big difference between living with their girlfriend and marrying her, even if you don't. So let's say he's like those other young men. What if he didn't want to get married?" Elias pressed. "Now, you're working as a waitress, you're living with a man, he won't marry you, and what if now, a baby comes along?"

"Daet!" Violet's eyes filled with tears. "Why are you doing this?"

She was so much more naive than she thought, and he knew this line of thinking was upsetting for her, but it would be much worse if she never considered it at all.

"Violet, I'm trying to show you how easy it is for things to get out of control," Elias said. "But the life you never wanted can start with the best of intentions, and your beautiful dreams for the future can slide away on you, and before you know it, you're in a place you never thought you'd be."

"I wouldn't do that!" Violet said.

"Good. I'm glad." He paused, and he wished he could just continue sheltering her, but there were things she needed to understand, especially now that she was old enough to long for that Englisher freedom. "But out there with the Englishers, you'd be alone. Choices you wouldn't make with a family all around you to help you out might be harder to avoid when you're on your own. Here in the Amish world, you'd have me and your grandparents and your aunts and uncles, your cousins, your friends, the bishop and elders—all people who care about you—looking out for your future…"

"And Delia?" Violet asked pointedly. "I'd have her, too, if you have your way?"

Aha. So maybe they were getting to part of the issue—the thought of a stepmother.

"Maybe," Elias said. "Maybe you'd have a stepmother who'd love you and give you advice and could help you navigate courting."

"And she'd tell you everything I did?" Violet said. "Like now?"

"Sometimes people caring about you means that they report back to your *daet* when they see you playing with something that could be dangerous," he agreed.

"But you don't even know Liam," she said, her voice shaking. "None of you do!"

"I don't," Elias agreed. "You're right. But neither do you, Violet. He's just a boy who gave you attention." He saw her expression close again, and he sighed. After one evening of talking, she *thought* she knew Liam. "I know how difficult life can be, and I'm trying to protect you."

"I'm not going to do anything silly," she said, and she took a step away. "So you don't have to worry about that."

But her definition of silly and his were very different. Violet turned toward the door. It looked like his opportunity to talk with her was closing. If only she could understand how very complicated and difficult the world could be.

"Let me tell you a story," Elias said.

Violet paused in her retreat. "I'm not a little girl anymore."

"Humor me," he said. "Come back and let me tell it."

Violet reluctantly returned to where he stood and she leaned against the rail again. So Elias turned back to grooming and began his tale.

"Once there was a boy who had a horse. It was a small horse, and he needed to sell it. So he brought his little horse to a farmer who was looking for a horse to plow his field. The farmer looked at the little horse and shook his head. He said, 'That horse is too small. I'd give you a hundred dollars for him. He's no good for farm work!'"

"Poor little horse," Violet said.

"I know. So then, the boy took his horse to a horse auction, and the auctioneer looked at him and said, 'That horse might be good for children to ride, if he was trained properly. You might be able to get a thousand dollars for him.'"

"That's better," Violet said.

"And the boy almost said yes," Elias said, shooting her a smile. "But then his grandfather said, 'Take that horse to the racing stables. And ask that horse breeder what he'd pay for him.' And so he did. And the horse breeder said, 'That horse has the makings of a fine racer. I'll pay you fifty thousand dollars right now!'"

"Oh!" Violet laughed, and her eyes widened.

"Do you know the moral?" he asked.

"Ask your grandfather before you sell a horse?"

Almost, but so far from what he wanted her to learn and to tuck away.

"You need to go to where people know your true value," Elias said. "Violet, you are worth all the love in a man's heart and his most faithful vow. You are. And you can have it! But just because you are worth your weight in gold doesn't mean every man will see that, or treat you accordingly. And that's what I'm trying to protect you from."

"That's what I want, too," Violet said earnestly. "But I don't want to be a farmer's wife. I don't want to be the woman who cooks and cleans and gets calluses on her hands from all the hard work. I want a husband who loves me for more than the work I do around the house. That's what I want."

Her bright gaze moved to the door again, and he could feel the whole world tugging at her heart, pulling her away from the world he'd raised her for. That big, heartless world wanted their tender, sheltered children. The world told them that the knowledge of good and evil was preferable to innocence. And he wished he had the words to fix all of this for her—to show her how it all fit together—but he kept coming up short.

"You can find that here with an Amish life," he said. "There are plenty of Amish men who aren't farmers, if that's your worry. I work at the canning plant. Your uncle and aunt own a restaurant. There are other options."

"It's not just about the job, Daet," she said with a long-suffering look on her face.

And he knew it wasn't, but she couldn't see the pitfalls waiting for her that he saw.

"I'm going to go help Mammi with dishes," Violet said.

He could talk and talk, but would she truly hear him? Or would she look back on these talks years from now and realize what he'd meant after she'd had her heart broken out there with all her freedom?

"All right," Elias said. "That's nice of you to help your *mammi*. I'll finish up out here."

Violet headed out the door and it clattered shut behind her. The horse nuzzled his hand, and Elias started brushing again, his mind tumbling over her words.

"I love my daughter for more than her cooking and cleaning, too," he murmured.

Elias loved Violet for who she was, and for her bright

smile. He loved her for her laughter and her silly jokes. He even loved her for her brooding teenage worries. He loved her for the depth of her heart and the height of her hopes. He'd loved her since her first newborn cries and would continue to love her into the future when he knew she'd leave his home and go start a life of her own and she'd no longer be under his careful protection.

But did she know that?

# Chapter Eight

Delia watched as Joseph's buggy disappeared onto the main road. She would follow him in her own buggy shortly.

Joseph had seemed different this time—more vulnerable and more helpless. Joseph and her mother had always maintained a very united front. Mamm had called the shots with parenting, and Joseph had backed her up with unswerving loyalty to her. But that relationship had very much been between Joseph and her mother. So to have Joseph come to her…it meant that Joseph was really, truly at the end of his rope.

Was Mamm going to be all right? She'd seen other women in the community dealing with aging parents, but somehow that had felt very far away for her. Until now. Things were starting to change around here, weren't they? The boys were growing up, but more than that, everyone else was growing older, too. Including Delia.

As Delia turned toward her own buggy, she saw Elias bend down and squeeze through the rungs of the fence, and somehow the sight of his tall strength was comforting. He carried a basket in one hand that he held aloft as he hopped on one foot, pulling his other boot over the rail.

"Good evening," he said. "I come bearing some baking from my mother."

Delia couldn't help but smile at that.

*"Danke,"* she said. "That's nice that she thought of me."

"Well, she's already mentally planning our wedding, so…this baking is really the least of it." He handed the basket over and she peeked inside to see three round loaves of bread. Those would be very helpful over the next couple of days.

"How disappointed will she be when they find out you weren't really courting me?" she asked.

"Quite. But take that as a compliment, and I think they'll understand why we did this. They can see how Violet has been struggling with things."

Delia hoped so. Elias paused, his warm gaze moving over her face, and she dropped her gaze under his sudden scrutiny.

"Are you all right? You look a bit shaken," he said.

She felt a rush of relief that he'd noticed.

"That was my stepfather just leaving," Delia said. "My *mamm* is…well, I don't know what is wrong with her exactly, but she needs to see a doctor."

Elias's expression clouded. "Can I help at all?"

Delia was about to say no, that she could handle this alone, but suddenly a wash of longing swamped her. She didn't want to do it all alone. She didn't want to be the only person providing solutions around here.

*"Yah,* actually," she said. "I wouldn't mind some help. I'm headed to see her now."

"Do you want me to drive you in my buggy?" he

asked. "I'll wait outside while you talk to her, but at least you won't have to worry about the ride and the hitching."

"That would be very nice."

More than nice. It would be a welcome relief.

"I'll just go hitch up," he said.

A few minutes later, Elias came down her drive in his buggy. He pulled up next to her and scooted over, then reached down, offering her his hand. She looked up at him and found his warm, friendly gaze locked on her.

Her heart skipped a beat, and before she could think better of it, she reached back, grasped his strong, warm hand, and he boosted her up into the seat next to him. He didn't let go of her hand right away, and when she looked up at him again, the warm look in his eyes had softened to something like melted chocolate. At least that was what it reminded her of—the chocolate she melted to cover caramels.

"You seem like this news has really shaken you," he said softly.

"It's…it's just that Mamm seems to be forgetting a lot—more than usual. She's messing up recipes and buying huge quantities of flour because she forgets she bought it already, and…Joseph is worried. And if Joseph is worried, that worries me."

Elias flicked the reins and the buggy started forward.

"I'm just going to go talk to her a bit, and hopefully convince her to go to a doctor's appointment," she said. "That's all I can really do at the moment. I'm hoping she listens to me."

Delia gave him the directions—out past the lake, west along the road that passed the old schoolhouse, and then down the first gravel drive by the third four-way stop.

They fell into silence as Elias navigated the buggy up the drive and onto the road.

"It's different when our parents get older, isn't it?" she asked. "They need us in new ways."

"*Yah*, mine are aging, too. My *daet* insists upon fixing things, even when it isn't reasonable. And I help him do it, because…I suppose I want him to be happy."

Delia nodded. *"Yah…"*

"But their health is strong, and that's a blessing. One day I'll be dealing with the same things, I'm sure. Everyone gets older."

"How is Violet?" Delia asked.

"I had a talk with her," he said.

"*Yah?* Did it go well?"

"I'm not sure…" He cast her a rueful look. "I think it will take more than one talk."

She understood that well enough, too.

"All we can do is our best, Elias," she said.

Elias reached over and took her hand in his, his warm fingers curling around hers. He seemed to have surprised himself, because he suddenly looked over at her, then down at their hands as if he hadn't quite meant to do that. She didn't mind, though. She gave his hand a gentle squeeze and a smile touched his lips.

"It helps to have a good friend, doesn't it?" he asked quietly.

"It truly does."

His hand was so reassuring in hers, reminding her of the comfort of having a man to lean on in difficult times. She'd been strong on her own for so long now, that she'd forgotten what it felt like to have a man's support. And Elias, in particular, was very nice to sit next to.

"Can I ask you something?" Elias asked.

"*Yah*, of course." She hoped that the heat in her cheeks didn't mean she was blushing.

"Why didn't you ride back with your stepfather?"

Delia sighed. "We don't have that kind of relationship, Joseph and I. I don't call him Daet, either. You see, I was fourteen when my *mamm* married him, and while he was never mean or anything, he was just…disinterested in us *kinner*. I called him Fadder until I got married, and then he told me that if I was more comfortable calling him Joseph, he didn't mind. And that's what I've called him ever since."

"It sounds difficult," Elias said.

"It isn't…well, maybe it is," she admitted. "I don't want to ever do that to my boys, you see. I don't want them to have a father in the home who only makes things harder for them."

"And they know it," Elias said.

"*Yah*, they know it," she agreed. "That's part of the problem, I suppose. They know that I don't want them to experience feeling unloved or uncared for, and they know I won't give them a stepfather who doesn't love them like he should. But I suppose it's difficult for any relationship to develop between my boys and another man while they fight every man who thinks I might make a good wife."

This time Elias squeezed her hand. "I think you'll figure it out. I really do. It might just take the right man."

She shot him a smile.

"He'll have to be quite the man—just about perfect, I'm afraid."

Elias just chuckled, and somehow, deep in her heart,

she realized that she'd started to hope that Elias might fit the bill. It was silly of her, because Elias was not looking for a wife currently, either! But if her boys would only settle down enough to consider having a new *daet* in their lives, a man like Elias—kind, strong, thoughtful—would be ever so nice to cook for.

But she had to check those fleeting hopes starting to flutter up inside her, and she slipped her hand out of his grip. Developing tender feelings for the man was not part of the plan! Elias looked over at her, and for a moment, she thought he almost looked hurt, but he took hold of the reins instead and put his eyes back on the road.

"Where are the boys tonight?" he asked.

Her hand felt so empty now.

"They've gone for pizza with their cousins," she said. "Where is Violet?"

"My *mamm* is showing her some keepsakes she has from her childhood," he replied. He was silent for a moment. "She did say something today about being worried about having a stepmother. She seemed angry about it."

"What part? Does she not like me, particularly?" Delia asked.

"No, I think she was upset that you told me about the Englisher boy," he said.

Delia winced. "*Yah*, she would be."

"You aren't the only one who told me about him, though," Elias said.

"That won't matter to her," Delia replied. "Maybe I'll be able to smooth things over with her yet. But she's right, you know."

"About what?"

"A stepmother will help in the raising of her, and she

wouldn't be keeping secrets from you, either. That's not right in a marriage. No secrets between a husband and wife."

"What do I do?" he asked.

"You keep that conversation going," she replied. "There will be a lot to talk about between the two of you, and she has to trust that her father will continue loving her just the same as he always did."

"*Danke* for the advice with her," he said, and he cast her a warm look again.

It was probably just as well that Elias wasn't here in Redemption for long, because given too much time with him, Delia was bound to fall for the man herself. And with all five of their combined *kinner* not ready for remarriages, there was no point in getting any of their hearts entangled.

But once Elias had Violet ready for some changes, he'd have no problem at all finding a lovely woman to share his life with. Elias would be very easy for any good woman to love.

Elias pulled up next to Joseph's buggy. A small, one-level house sat on a sparse section of land. There was a large chicken coop behind the house, and he could hear the flutter and cluck of the birds as he reined his horse in. The older man had already unhitched, and was heading back from the stable, his rubber boots squelching through the wet ground around a water pump. Joseph shot Elias a quizzical look.

Right. Why was he here during an obviously private family affair? He could almost feel the man's questions, but Elias didn't regret coming. Delia needed support, too, even though she'd come to offer hers.

Delia's finger plucked at her dress, betraying some nervous energy. She wasn't comfortable here—he could tell that much.

"I'll just wait out here, obviously," Elias said to Delia.

She nodded, and her hands stilled. "*Danke*, Elias. I don't know how long I'll be…"

"It doesn't matter," he replied. "Take all the time you need, and I'll drive you home when you're ready."

He meant it with all his heart. He could wait as long as she needed, but he wasn't going to leave without her unless she specifically asked him to.

"You are a sweet man, Elias," Delia said, her eyes misting, and his heart skipped a beat. If they were alone, he'd be tempted to lean in and press his lips against her forehead—an image of doing just that rose so forcefully in his mind that he had to muscle it back—but Joseph was out there watching them. As if that was the only reason, although it was the first one to come to mind. The truth was, Delia wasn't really his to kiss, was she? The fact that their courtship wasn't real was getting harder and harder to remember. He was starting to fool himself.

So instead, Elias reached out and caught her hand in his. He gave it a gentle squeeze, and her smile was reward enough. She slipped out of the buggy, and met her stepfather in front of the house.

Elias watched them talk quietly for a moment, and then the side door opened, revealing Delia's white-haired mother. The three of them went back into the house together, and the screen door bounced shut behind them.

Why on earth had he held her hand like that? Well,

maybe it was better to ask why he'd allowed himself to do it. He knew why he'd wanted to—because Delia was beautiful and comforting and sweet... But it was foolish. *Yah*, they were supposed to appear like they were courting for the sake of the *kinner*, but he wasn't actually supposed to court her! He knew he shouldn't be allowing himself to feel more, but he was. He wasn't sure where that left him.

Elias let out a long, slow breath. *Yah*, it would seem that he was feeling more for Delia Swarey than he should be. He wanted to comfort her, to support her, to help her out of her troubles. He wanted to be her answer in her difficult times—and when a man's heart went in that direction, it was dangerous indeed.

Elias had a pocket-size German Bible, and he brought it out and started to read. He had gotten through most of the book of Matthew by the time Delia came back out again. She paused on the step and said a few words to Joseph, and then the door shut behind her as she came back to the buggy.

Elias tucked his Bible away again and scooted over to give her a hand back up into the seat next to him. She had a ball of pink yarn in her hands, and she stroked it absently.

"You're ready to head home?" he asked.

"*Yah*, I am," she said, and exhaled a shaky breath.

Elias flicked the reins and brought the buggy around. He leaned forward, but no one was on the step or in the window. As they went back up the bumpy drive, he reached for her hand again, and she reached back, clasping his hand fervently.

"I convinced Mamm to go to the doctor," Delia said.

"That's good."

"She's upset with me, though. She thinks I'm not be-
lieving her. She sees this as betrayal—by both me and
Joseph."

He had no idea how to make that better, so he squeezed
her hand, then released it as he took the reins and guided
the horse back onto the road.

"Did you see evidence of her…slipping?" he asked.

"*Yah.* She didn't remember things—like my birth-
day, or my youngest son's name. She kept calling him
the little one. It was confusing. Joseph said that this
was a bad patch, but at least I was able to see it. Mamm
needs help."

They headed back the way they'd come, and Delia
leaned back in the seat. Elias stole a look at her, and her
gaze was trained on the road, worry lines creasing her
brow. She ran her fingers gently over that pink ball of
soft yarn.

"The boys have a key to get back inside," Delia said.
"And all four of them are together. I think we could take
the long way home, if you don't mind."

"I don't mind at all," he murmured, and he felt a rush
of gratitude that he was able to offer at least this much. He
wanted to take her hand again, but he knew he shouldn't
do that.

He looked over at her instead, and he saw tears welling in her eyes.

"Delia?" he said gently.

"She didn't remember my little girl…" Delia's chin
trembled, and she wiped at her cheeks. "I'm sorry, it's
just that my *mamm* helped me through the loss of a
baby girl, and… She had started knitting a little pink

sweater for the baby when I was pregnant, and when I lost the baby, she stopped knitting. That unfinished sweater stayed on the top of her knitting basket always. But she forgot, and she thought she'd made a mistake in the counting, or something, and she ripped it apart." Delia looked down at the ball of yarn. "She'd forgotten everything, and we caught her unraveling it and wrapping the yarn up into a ball."

"Oh, Delia," he murmured.

"I took the ball of yarn—I shouldn't have. It won't make any of it better, but—" Her chin trembled, and a tear slipped down her cheek.

Something inside him burned hot, and he wanted to fix this—somehow. It was his male way of thinking— he saw the woman he cared for crying, and he wanted to kick down doors and make someone pay. But there was no one to pay for this...

Ahead, Elias saw a side road that he knew led down to a creek. He took the turn and then reined in by the babbling water. The shade was cool, and the low sunlight slanted like gold through the trees.

Elias didn't say anything else. He just moved over on the bench seat, slipped his arms around Delia's shoulders and pulled her solidly against his chest. He could feel her warm tears wetting his shirt. He had no words for this kind of pain, but he was glad she shared it with him. He ran his hand across her shaking shoulders, and he pressed a kiss on the top of her hair that was exposed before her *kapp* covered the rest. How much pain did this woman carry around with her, unknown to anyone else?

When Delia leaned back, her face was blotchy, and her eyes were red. She sniffled, and he wished that there was something more he could do to make any of this easier for her.

"I hope I don't seem like I'm maladjusted or something, but this is why I wanted to spend some time with Violet," Delia said, dabbing at her nose with a handkerchief. "A girl around the farm, working with the boys— I don't know, it felt nice."

"You don't have to feel bad about that," he said. "I always wanted more *kinner*, and spending time with your boys has filled a hole in my heart, too. So no guilt over enjoying time with my daughter."

*"Danke,"* she said with a faint smile. She turned her gaze down to the ball of yarn in her lap. "I lost my little girl, and I'm losing my mother, too…"

"She needs a doctor," he said firmly. "She's not lost yet. I'm sure they can help. But I know what you mean. Time marches on, doesn't it?"

"Since when did we become the people in charge in our broader families, Elias?" she asked, shaking her head. "Since when did we become the ones who must come up with all the solutions?"

"I guess we know how little prepared our own parents felt at our age, don't we?" he said.

She met his gaze and a smile touched her lips. "I suppose so. We all rely on Gott more than our *kinner* ever guess."

"Amen to that," Elias said, and he took her hand once more. Her fingers felt cool and delicate in his grasp. "Delia, I know this is all overwhelming, but you're a good mother and a good daughter and…a good friend to me. Many people are thankful for you in their lives. I know that for a fact."

"How is it you know the right things to say?" she asked softly.

"I was just…being honest," he admitted feebly.

"Even that…" She wiped at her cheek again. "I thought I'd have more wisdom by now, Elias."

"Me, too," he said. "I'm not sure how much wisdom I've got, but I do have perspective. And I know a good woman when I meet her."

"Raising four boys alone isn't easy," she said. "And now my *mamm* will need my help—and Joseph, too."

"I wish I could stay longer," he said. The words were out before he could even think them through. He did wish he could stay longer—just spend a few more weeks or even months next door to this lovely woman. He wanted to get to know her better and lend a hand where he could.

Delia dropped her gaze then, and she pressed her lips together.

"Did I say something wrong?" he asked.

"Elias, I'm…" Her cheeks colored. "You've been very kind and very good to me. But I'm…" She swallowed. "What I'm trying to say is that I'm not used to getting this kind of attention from a man. And while other women might be able to keep their feelings in check, I'm finding it hard to—" She turned away. "You are a handsome man. You must know that. That's not me flattering you—I'm just trying to point out that… Oh, I'm sounding like a fool."

She sounded nothing like a fool. She sounded honest and sweet and like maybe she had been feeling the same way he had.

"Am I crossing lines, Delia?" he asked cautiously.

He'd promised both her and her son that he wouldn't do that.

"No!" she said. "Maybe... I don't know!" She turned back toward him. "All I know is that I'm enjoying this time with you more than we agreed to."

"I am, too," he said, and he caught her gaze.

"Then we'd better be careful!" she said, her voice becoming firm. "We've got five *kinner* between us who are supposed to learn about proper courting that doesn't cross lines and leaves no hearts broken. They're supposed to get used to the idea of a stepparent, not get dragged into something messy!"

Elias licked his lips and nodded. "You're right."

"I'm sorry that I'm not at my best," she said. "I'm normally a little more pulled together."

"Delia, you're perfect," he said.

A smile touched her lips. "Oh, Elias, you'd better stop with that sweet talking."

"I keep telling you," he said with a low laugh, "I'm not trying to sweet-talk you. I'm just telling you how I see it."

But her warning was a wise one. Somehow, he'd started out wanting to give Violet the benefit of Delia's advice, and instead he'd let himself get attached to her. It was happening a little too easily. With every other woman, his armor had been up. But with Delia, he didn't seem to have any armor.

"I'll take you home now," he said. "Will you be all right?"

"*Yah*, I'm feeling better," she said. "*Danke*, Elias."

His name on her tongue sounded sweet, but he didn't let himself dwell on that. He'd best get home, too. He was here to help his parents move house, not to get his heart battered.

Besides, her boys would be home soon, and he needed time with his own daughter.

The *kinner* had to come first.

# Chapter Nine

As Elias pulled up to the Swarey farm, Violet stood outside on the grass, her feet bare and her gaze steely. He knew that look, and Elias couldn't help but sigh. The boys had returned, too, from their supper out with cousins. They sat outside on the step looking bored, and all five sets of teenage eyes turned toward the buggy as he reined in the horse.

"The boys don't look happy," Delia murmured.

"Neither does my daughter."

They exchanged a look, and he tied off the reins. The *kinner* might not look happy, but they didn't know the pain their *mamm* carried in her heart tonight, either. "Is there anything else I can do to make your evening easier?"

"No, you've done so much already," Delia replied. "I'll be all right. *Danke* for being here for me today. It was kind."

"It's where I wanted to be," he said.

Delia dropped her gaze. He sounded like he was flirting, he knew, but he wasn't. Of course he'd help her! She was his parents' neighbor, an old friend…a new friend. And she was starting to feel like a confidante, too, and someone he wanted to stay in contact with once he headed home again… But they had an irritated audience, and there was no time to say more tonight.

"You weren't home when we got here," Moses said, standing up from his seat on the step. "Where were you?"

The last thing Delia needed tonight was her sons talking back to her. She had enough on her shoulders.

"Hey," Elias said, letting his voice carry. "I know you boys don't like me stepping out with your *mamm*, but you watch how you talk to her."

"That was rather rude, Moses," Ezekiel said.

"Sorry, Mamm," the boy muttered.

"I had to go help your *mammi*," Delia said. "She's not feeling herself lately, and Dawdie Joseph asked for my help."

Expressions changed then. The boys jumped up and those angry looks changed to worry. They'd have a lot to talk about as a family that wasn't really Elias's business.

He allowed his fingers to linger over Delia's hand, and she cast him a grateful look, then pulled her fingers free and jumped down from the buggy.

"I thought you had a key to get in the house," Delia said as she made her way toward the porch.

"We do. We came outside to wait for you. We thought you were on a date," Thomas said, and he cast a somewhat annoyed look in Elias's direction. Apparently, all was not forgiven with those suspenders, after all.

"Without telling us!" Moses interjected, his voice trailing off as Delia and her boys headed into the house.

Violet came over to the buggy and hoisted herself up. She landed with a huff on the seat next to him.

"That was a date, wasn't it?" she said.

"Violet, I gave her a ride to her mother's home. That's it."

But was it? Was he lying to his daughter tonight as well as to himself? Because he'd certainly been more than her ride. He'd been her friend and her comfort, too. Still, *kinner* couldn't understand these complexities.

"What's wrong with her *mamm*?" Violet asked, her tone softening.

"It's private family business for them," Elias said, flicking the reins to turn the buggy around. "Can I trust your discretion?"

Violet's shoulders straightened. "Of course, Daet."

"Good. Well, Delia's *mamm* is having trouble with her memory—a lot of trouble. She's going to need to go to a doctor and hopefully the doctor can help her, but it sounds serious to me. And sometimes when older people are struggling, they blame the ones trying to help them."

"So Delia's *mamm* is mad at her for trying to help?" Violet asked.

"It seems that way."

"Poor Delia…" Violet murmured.

"*Yah*, poor Delia," he agreed. Poor Delia, indeed. She took care of so much all by herself, and she never seemed to have a moment just to rest or get her balance back. "Delia will be talking to the boys about it tonight, I'm sure," he went on. "They shouldn't hear it from you."

"I'm not going to say anything," Violet said. "I'm not a kid."

Elias smiled faintly. Because she was a kid, but he had to admit that she was quickly growing up.

"I hope when I'm old, I don't give you a hard time for trying to help me," he said.

"You'd better not!" Violet said, but she cast him an impish little smile.

As he guided the buggy into his parents' drive, he looked out over that familiar landscape. He'd grown up here, and while his sister Mary would be raising her own *kinner* in this little house, this did feel like the end of an era.

"I'll get older, you know," Elias said as he reined in the horse. "It's a fact of life. And no one knows how that will go. Mammi and Dawdie are strong and healthy still. They need my help, but not as much as Delia's *mamm* will need. And when I get old, I don't know if I'll be strong and healthy—Gott willing—or if I'll decline faster."

"Daet, don't talk about that. You're the strongest man I know!"

"Right now, I am." He turned toward her. "Violet, I will always do my best to take care of you. But these are the things I think about. If you do as you've been threatening to do, and you leave the Amish life, I'll grow old alone. I won't have you here to help me when I need it."

Violet's eyes misted. "I'd come back and take care of you! I could come every morning and check on you when you're old."

"Not from town. It's too far away."

"Then I'll live closer!"

"How?" He shook his head. "Violet, I understand you wanting your own life. That yearning you feel to get some space and to spread your wings is natural. Gott built us with that drive inside of us so that we'll get married and have our own families. But leaving the faith… I've told you all this time what you'd be giving up in your own life. But I'm also thinking about what I'd lose if you went away."

His voice caught in his throat, and he swallowed hard.

"Oh, Daet…" Violet's eyes misted again. "I'd go before I was baptized, and they could never shun me then. I'd come back—I promise I'd come back!"

But Elias knew that if she left, it wouldn't be so easy. She'd have a life, a job, a home…a family. And he'd be far away—a long drive in a car and nothing very conveniently close. Maybe her husband wouldn't like coming out to Amish Country. Maybe if she came it would cause problems in her marriage. Life could be infinitely more complicated than youths imagined it would be. And he'd miss her more than she'd ever miss him—it was just a simple fact. And she'd only understand a parent's love after she had a beautiful, bouncing little girl or boy of her own. But he didn't want to give her a load of guilt, either. Maybe Delia was right and this would be a very long conversation yet.

"Let's unhitch," Elias said.

"I'll help."

He cast her a mildly surprised look. She didn't often like helping unhitch the buggy, but he was glad for her company all the same. For the next few minutes, they worked on buckles and getting the horse freed from his burden. Then he led the horse to the pasture so he could graze a while.

Elias leaned against the fence and removed his straw hat, letting the air cool his neck and his sweat-dampened hair.

"You say you'll be all alone without me," Violet said, leaning against the fence next to him. "But if you marry

Delia, you'd have her and her *kinner* and whatever other babies you had. You won't miss me that much."

"Would it be so terrible to have a family—you, me and others we could both love?" he asked.

"I know it's selfish," she said in a low voice, "but I just wanted it to be me and you. For a while more, at least. Mamm hasn't been gone that long, and I miss her so much… A stepmother isn't going to want to talk about Mamm, is she?"

Elias's heart squeezed. "Your *mamm* was wonderful…"

"I know," Violet said, and a tear leaked down her cheek. "Do you remember how she used to make those silly puns all the time?"

"*Yah*… They were terrible, weren't they?"

They laughed sadly, and Violet tipped her head against his shoulder like she used to years ago. He planted a kiss against her head, and tears rose in his eyes.

"I understand if you want a new wife," Violet said. "But it's hard for me to move on to a new *mamm*. A wife and *mamm* are very different, aren't they?"

So much insight in one young teenager. Maybe she was more grown-up than he'd given her credit for. He heaved out a slow sigh.

"I'm not courting Delia," he said quietly.

"What?" Violet lifted her head.

"I'm not really courting Delia," he said, and he cast his daughter an apologetic look. "The thing is, Delia and I do want to get married again one day—not to each other, but we want that. And her boys are standing guard over her. We thought if you *kinner* thought we were courting, that we could open up some conversations about remarriage and moving on from our grief."

"So…you lied?" Violet whispered.

"We…didn't really. We said we were getting to know each other. Which was true. And we let you believe it was more."

"That's a lie!" Violet said.

"I'm sorry," he said. "I was hoping that you'd see that there is romance possible here in the Amish world. I thought that you might like Delia, and that you might feel comfortable talking to her where you weren't comfortable talking to me."

"Except it wasn't real," she retorted. "So, Delia doesn't really want to marry you?"

He shook his head. "No. She doesn't."

Violet heaved out a breath. "Well, good."

"I'm sorry if I just made things worse," he said. "My intentions were good. Do you know what I think?"

"What?" She cast him a wary look.

"I think you want to go English because an Amish life without your *mamm* feels unbearable and wrong."

Violet's chin trembled. "It does…"

"But there is still life and beauty here, Violet," he said earnestly. "We can still be happy! Your *mamm* would have wanted you to be happy here, with your own people."

"I don't want to watch you loving someone else, Daet," she said.

"Not even eventually?" he asked. "Not now, but…one day? It would be different, but we could still be happy!"

"You could still be happy." Violet wiped a tear off her cheek.

She was still young, and maybe her ideas would change yet. They'd started talking, hadn't they?

"You don't have to worry about that right now," he

said. "Delia and I are only friends. We bonded over having *kinner* we love more than anything. So...don't worry about it right now, all right?"

He put an arm around her shoulder and tugged her into a hug. Only a friend... *Yah*, that was the plan they'd made when this started, but he was feeling his heart pulling toward Delia all the same. Maybe as a man and a father, it was his duty to shoulder the loneliness that came with being a widower so that his daughter could feel safe and secure.

"Okay, Daet," Violet said, and she leaned into his side. He felt a rush of relief mingled with fatherly protectiveness. He had to show Violet a happy life here with their people.

But if his courtship with Delia had been a real one, it would have been a sweet one. Maybe he'd let himself pretend a little too well, because while Violet seemed to be feeling better, his heart was starting to ache.

That evening, Delia sat the boys down and they talked about Mammi's need to see a doctor.

"Will she be okay?" Aaron asked, squinting across the table. "Like, is there a pill or something to fix it?"

"Boys, I don't know how to answer that," Delia said slowly. "I hope so. But sometimes as people get older, things change. It's possible that Mammi's memory is going to be affected for the rest of her life. And if that is the case, then we will just have to love her as she is. Sometimes forgetting makes her grumpy, too, Dawdie Joseph told me. So if that happens, don't get your feelings hurt. Mammi is doing the very best she can. Do you understand?"

The boys did understand. They had big hearts, and they loved their grandparents dearly. Zeke's *mamm* and *daet* had already passed away, but Mammi Linda and Dawdie Joseph were still a big part of their lives. They visited often, and Dawdie Joseph taught them a fair amount about woodworking. Mammi Linda made them their very favorite sugar cookies, too. And the boys all agreed that they'd do their best to help Mammi and wouldn't feel bad if she forgot things.

As Delia lay in bed that night listening to the chirp of crickets outside the window, she silently prayed for strength and guidance.

*Gott, please help me as I raise my boys*, she prayed. *Guide their steps, and their hearts. Show me what they need most. And, Gott, please help my* mamm...

She prayed through her list of people who needed Him. Her mother, Joseph, the doctor... She prayed for her friends and her neighbors and for dear, sweet Elias, who had been such a source of patience and strength.

That was where she suddenly stopped. Elias... She rubbed her hands over her face. Elias had been such a help these last few days—more than he even thought. True, they were helping their children to accept the idea of a stepparent, but just having Elias around had made everything easier to bear. She felt stronger with him by her side. Even when she ended up crying in his arms. But the problem was, she wasn't as strong as she should be, because when Elias wasn't around, she'd started missing him and wishing she had an excuse to see him again sooner. The thought of him going back to Indiana was really starting to hurt. What was she, a teenage girl?

*Thank You for sending Elias when I needed him most,*

Delia prayed. *And help me to keep my emotions in check, Gott. I seem to be feeling more for him than I should.*

And while Gott didn't seem to be dousing her tenderness toward Elias, slumber did overtake her. She had a deep, dreamless sleep and awoke the next morning more refreshed than she'd been in a very long time.

The next day was a busy one. Another flower truck was scheduled to arrive, and they all got to work early. Violet arrived to help about half an hour after the boys started work, and Delia sent Ezekiel and Violet to start filling buckets of long-stemmed blooms.

The work passed quickly, and by the time the truck arrived, they had most of the flowers ready to load up. Working together, they saw the truck loaded and forms signed, and in good time the truck crept back up the drive to deliver the flower shipment to florists in the city.

"*Danke*, all of you," Delia said. "You've worked so hard, and that is our last big shipment for another couple of weeks. So it won't be quite so hectic."

But the *kinner* weren't acting like they usually did after a big shipment was loaded and sent on its way. They looked down at their shoes and scuffed their toes in the dirt.

"I've got cookies in the house," Delia said hopefully. "I think we all deserve a treat, don't you?"

"Mamm, you lied to us," Moses said loudly.

"Moses!" Ezekiel snapped. "Enough!"

"Well, she did!" Moses's face went red. "She lied!"

Delia's heart hammered to a stop. "Excuse me?"

"Are you really courting Violet's *daet*?" Thomas asked quietly. "Or was it a trick?"

The *kinner* all looked at her pointedly, and Delia felt her cheeks heat.

"I take it your *daet* talked to you about this, Violet?" Delia asked.

Violet's ears blazed red and she took a step backward. "*Yah*. He told me."

"Okay…" Delia sighed. "Then I think we need to talk."

"So, are you two courting or not?" Aaron asked. "Because you said—"

"I *said* we were getting to know each other," Delia said firmly. "And that was true. I *said* we were spending time together—"

"But you also talked to us about getting a new step-*daet* one of these days," Moses said.

"They wanted us to think they were courting so we'd get used to the idea, and probably be relieved when they didn't get married," Violet said.

"Is that it?" Ezekiel asked, meeting Delia's gaze. He looked disappointed. Sad. Let down.

"Something like that," she agreed. Somehow, now it seemed a little silly. Especially with her four boys looking at her like that.

"I think I should go home now…" Violet said. "If that's okay, Delia."

"*Yah*, Violet, you go on home," Delia said. "And I am sorry, dear."

"It's okay," Violet said. "It worked—I'm relieved."

That stung more than it should, and Delia felt a sudden mist of tears in her vision. She blinked it back and gestured toward the house.

"Come on, boys," Delia said. "Let's go talk."

The boys headed toward the side door of the house,

and Violet started a brisk walk back toward her grand-parents' home, her head down and her white *kapp* gleam-ing in the sunlight. Delia watched the girl go, and her heart tugged after her. Violet was angry, no doubt. And like she'd said, she was relieved. But Violet was a sweet girl under all her angst, and she deserved to have a good talk about this, too. Delia's instinct was to pull the girl inside with her own boys and include her in their talk about all of this, but they weren't actually a family, were they? That was Elias's place, and she needed to focus on her own boys, and let Elias do the same for his daughter.

She and Elias could talk about this later—and that thought was a comforting one. Maybe he'd have some insights into how boys thought that might help her navi-gate this in the coming weeks. And maybe just talking about it with Elias would make her feel better, too. He was just that kind of man.

The boys trudged in the side door, and Delia followed them. They sat down at the table—their usual talking spot—and she brought a plate of cookies she'd been sav-ing for a snack today and put it into the center. None of the boys even looked at the cookies—not even Moses. Delia couldn't help feeling a little rejected. They were obviously angry.

"Doesn't anyone want a cookie?" Delia asked.

She was met with silence.

"All right," Delia said, taking her seat. "Let's talk."

"How come you lied?" Moses demanded.

"I didn't mean to lie, exactly," Delia said. "I wanted you to start thinking about what it would be like for me to be seriously courted again."

"We've already thought about it," Aaron muttered. "It's not like this would have been the first time."

"*Yah*, but you've chased off every single man who's tried!" Delia said. "Don't you boys realize that you'll grow up? You'll get married. You'll move away from me, and I'll be left on my own. I'd like to have someone to grow old with."

"You will be left on your own," Ezekiel said. "That's what worries us. You've told us all countless times that who you marry is a sober choice. Marriage is for the rest of your life. And we know we'll move away, Mamm! That's the problem. If you marry a man who isn't kind to you or who doesn't love you like he should, then you're stuck with him for the rest of your life, and we won't always be here to protect you."

"Protect me?" Delia said.

"*Yah,*" Thomas said seriously. "We know it's our job to keep you safe, Mamm. And you're not so tough as you want us to believe."

"I am too!" she retorted. "I'm your mother, and don't you forget that I'm the parent here. You are the children."

"We hear you cry." Aaron's eyes welled with tears, and his brothers fell silent.

"What?" Delia whispered.

"Late at night," Moses said, nodding. "We hear you cry sometimes, and we promised each other that we'd never let a man make you cry—not ever."

This time, no one shushed Moses, and her sons all looked up. Moses had struck on their main motivation, it seemed. And he'd spoken for them all. Delia sucked in a wavering breath.

"Boys…" But she felt her chin quiver then, and she

shook her head. "You beautiful *kinner*. Do you know how much I love you?"

*"Yah..."* they muttered.

"Well, I do! And I know you want to keep me safe, but it really is my job to keep you safe. That's how Gott intended it."

"Gott also intended for men to protect women," Ezekiel said. "And for *kinner* to help their parents when they get old. Like you are with Mammi."

"I'm not old yet!" Delia protested.

"You kind of are," Moses replied with a weak shrug, and Delia couldn't help but laugh. Maybe to an eleven-year-old she was!

"But it's okay, because you aren't marrying him," Thomas cut in. "Ezekiel talked to him, and he said Elias promised not to hurt you. I guess that was true."

"Elias didn't tell me that..." she murmured.

"That was between men," Ezekiel replied. "But I can see that he was telling the truth. He couldn't hurt you because you were never actually courting."

"That's true," Delia said. They hadn't been court-ing. But somehow, her heart was getting involved all the same—her lesson in proper courting not turning out as she'd expected. Maybe it never could have been so simple or straight. Maybe she should be a little more careful with her own heart!

"Here is the thing, boys," Delia said slowly. "I want to get married again one day. I'm lonely, and when you're older, you'll understand what I mean by that. I'd like to have a husband to cook for again. I'd like to have a husband to stand proudly with me when your engage-ments are announced on Service Sunday, and to drive in the buggy with me to come visit you on a weekend. I want a companion, someone who will grow old with me. I want that."

The boys were silent, but the tension was gone now.

"And while that won't be Elias, I would like to find a man who I can trust to be a good step*daet* to all of you and a good husband to me. I know it's a tall order to fill, but I'll have to be looking seriously at what a man has to offer, and I need you four to stop chasing those men off."

"Even if they aren't good enough?" Aaron asked.

"I'm asking that you give them a chance, and—" She saw their gazes hardening. "Okay, how about this? If I agree that the man isn't good enough, I'll let you four at him."

The boys started to smile then, and she laughed a little. "But please, stop chasing them away before I can even get to know them!"

"Just promise us that you won't marry a man who will boss you around," Ezekiel said.

"Or say mean things when he's hungry and tired," Aaron added.

"Or who doesn't think your jokes are funny," Moses said.

"I'll do even better than that," Delia said. "I won't marry a man who isn't good to me and good to you, too. And I won't marry a man who won't think you four are just as wonderful as I do. Because I couldn't face the rest of my life with a man who didn't see just how kind, thoughtful, talented and wonderful you boys are!"

"But what if that man makes you cry?" Thomas asked. "What then?"

"Let's play it by ear, okay?" she said. "But I think

our family could make room for a step*daet*, if he were the right man—don't you?"

The boys squirmed, then looked at Ezekiel, who sat motionless, his lips pursed.

"But I thought it seemed real, Mamm," Moses interjected. "Elias seemed to really like you, and you laughed a lot when Elias was around. Like you liked him, too, or something."

"I do like him," she replied. "He's my friend."

"I thought you liked him, like a boyfriend," Moses said. "I'm glad you don't really."

Her boys—her wonderful, protective, kind boys... She loved them more than they'd ever know. She nudged the plate of cookies closer to Aaron and Thomas.

"Have a cookie," she said softly.

And this time, they reached for a cookie. Moses stretched across the table on his belly to reach one, too, and then Delia slid the plate over to Ezekiel. He accepted a cookie with a boyish smile.

They were growing up, but they weren't grown yet. And a cookie could still make things better.

But her own problem remained. The courtship had been fake, but it had started to feel awfully real to her. She never should have let that happen.

## Chapter Ten

Elias lifted a box up into the wagon, then hopped up after it to get it settled in the right spot. This was the last wagonload to go over to Dina's home where the newly built *dawdie hus* was waiting.

Elias's brother-in-law, a couple of cousins and two men from the community had been there packing up the first wagonload that morning, and this was the last of his parents' personal items to be carried out to their new home.

"Here's another one," his father said, putting another box on the wagon bed.

Elias packed it with the others.

"I'm leaving the gardening equipment for your sister," his father said. "And your *mamm* has some bags of linens and all that, but I think we're about done."

It was rather sad to see the last of his parents' possessions so efficiently packed up and carried off, as if the very heart of this place was that easy to replace. His whole childhood had been here, and while his sister, Mary, was taking over the place, it would be different. His nieces and nephews would grow up here—a whole new generation of *kinner*. He was glad it would stay with the family, but it was a goodbye in a way, too.

He looked over in the direction of the Swarey farm, and he spotted his daughter coming in his direction. She was walking briskly, and he couldn't see any sign of the Swarey family—at least not from his vantage point. The truck that had been there earlier was gone now, and he hadn't heard it leave.

"Hi, Daet," Violet said. "Can I help?"

"Aren't you supposed to be working with Delia today?" he asked.

"We're done."

"Just…done? There's nothing else to be done?"

"The delivery truck came already," she said. "We're done now."

He shaded his eyes and looked over toward the farm. Normally he'd see one of the boys around, or Delia marching across the farmyard in her rubber boots. But everything looked still.

"Okay…" he said. "Great. Um, Mammi has some bags of linens that need to be carried over here. They might be heavy, though. See what you can do."

Elias had slept terribly the night before. He'd felt like he'd succeeded with Violet in their talk last night, but his heart had felt strangely sorrowful. He knew what grief felt like, and this had been just like that—an aching sadness for something lost. For someone lost.

But Delia wasn't lost. She was running a farm next door. If he wanted to, he could march right over and knock on her door. He could see her easily enough. She wasn't gone like Wanda was gone, and yet he was grieving this silly fake relationship. They'd been clear. Delia had been clearer! This was to help the *kinner* work through some of their deeper issues, not to actually start a romance.

And that was what he'd repeatedly told himself last night. It hadn't helped. He'd even woken up to read his Bible, hoping to find some peace in a familiar passage, but every time he opened the book, he stumbled across the Song of Solomon, or the story of Ruth. When he flipped to the New Testament, it was Joseph being told by the angel that he shouldn't be afraid to take Mary as his wife.

So he'd shut his Bible and gone back to bed. Obviously, deep in his heart somewhere, he'd starting longing for something more with Delia, and he couldn't help but feel foolish. And he'd prayed that Gott would help him to think sensibly about all of this. But it seemed that Gott wasn't going to remove his feelings so easily.

So today, tired and a little out of sorts because he'd only gotten about four hours of proper sleep the night before, Elias had set to work helping his parents pack up the last of their belongings.

"Oh, son!" his mother called from the side door. "Could I talk to you a moment?"

Elias hopped down from the back of the wagon and headed over to where his mother waited for him.

"I borrowed these garbage bags from Delia this morning. You don't think you could bring them over to her, do you?" She lowered her voice. "If that isn't going to be too awkward…"

"Mamm, it wasn't a real relationship," he said with a forced smile. "This isn't a breakup. There's no awkwardness. I count Delia as a good friend, and I'd be happy to return them for you."

More than happy. He found himself feeling oddly relieved. At least now he had a reason to go over there and see her and prove to himself that everything was fine between them.

"Come along, Judith," his father called. "Time to get this wagon moving."

"I'll be along shortly with the buggy," Elias told his mother. "I'll see you soon."

His father helped his mother up onto the front seat, and Violet hopped up next to them. His mother put an arm around Violet's waist to keep a good hold on her, and Violet laughed. It was a light, happy sound that he hadn't heard in years. He couldn't help smiling at the three of them, and the wagon rumbled off down the drive, the two draft horses plodding evenly along with the heavy load behind them.

He looked over at the box of garbage bags waiting on the step. It was just past one, and when he looked over toward the Swarey farm again, he spotted Aaron and Thomas heading out toward the fields again, dragging a long black hose behind them.

Elias should probably let Delia know that Violet knew the truth. Maybe she'd be ready to let her boys in on the ruse, too. It seemed to help get him and Violet talking, at the very least.

When he got to the Swarey farm, he knocked on the side door. There was no answer, so he left the box on the porch and headed out to see if he could spot Delia. The door to the greenhouse opened, and she appeared in the doorway with a bucket in one hand and a pair of clippers in the other. She waved with the clippers, and he angled his steps in her direction.

"Hi," Delia said, and she led the way into the greenhouse. It was hot inside, and a little humid. She sat on a stool in front of a potted shrub, and began to trim the plant with the clippers, leaves falling to the floor around her.

"My parents have taken the last load to my sister's place," he said.

Delia stopped her work and spun around on the stool to face him. "So…they're gone? I thought they were leaving later this evening. I was going to say goodbye to them before they left—" She winced. "But they're gone?"

"I mean, they'll be five miles down the road," he said with a reassuring smile. "You could pop by and see them anytime, and they'd be thrilled to see you."

"True." Her smile slipped. "I feel like I've been a terrible neighbor."

"Not true," he replied. "I just brought back a box of garbage bags my mother borrowed from you. It's on the side porch. My parents think you're wonderful. You know what they say—if you want to know if you're a good neighbor, ask your neighbor."

"Right…" Delia met his gaze. "Did Violet tell you what happened?"

"No…" In fact, she'd been a little evasive.

"Violet told my boys that you and I aren't really courting, and they were…hurt, mostly." She pressed her lips together, but they still trembled a little. So Violet had told them.

"I'm sorry she did that. I told her where things really stood with us, but I hadn't wanted her to tell the boys anything."

"They were so hurt that I'd do that to them."

"Do what, exactly?" he asked. Because he was ready to defend Delia!

"Let them believe there was more between us," she said. "My youngest said I lied. And...honestly? If they'd misled me, I'd have said the same thing."

"Delia..." he said gently.

"No, no," she said. "Don't try and make me feel better."

"Did you talk things through yet?" he asked.

"We had a good talk," she said. "They agreed to let me get to know some men and stop chasing them off first. My boys only wanted to protect me."

"I thought you didn't want their protection," he said.

"I don't..." Her cheeks suddenly bloomed pink, and she dropped her gaze. "Elias, I have a confession to make."

"Oh?" He stepped closer, and she refused to raise her eyes.

"It was starting to feel real—our courtship—to me." She looked up then, and embarrassment was written all over her face.

"For me, too," he said, and relief rushed through him. He wasn't the only one! "I was feeling so foolish, because spending that time with you and facing off with your boys and..." He smiled hopefully. "It was feeling awfully real to me, too. I started looking forward to seeing you and getting your advice, and..." He was saying too much, so he stopped talking, and he caught her hand. It just felt natural to reach out and take her hand in his, and she stepped a little closer.

"It did start to feel real, didn't it?" A smile touched her lips. "That might have scared you a bit."

"Not scared at all," he replied.

It had felt natural to open up to her, to hold her hand, to hold her close…and he found some powerful, testosterone-driven part of him that wanted to make sure no other man held her like that. Only him.

"Maybe it was all of these hard things coming together at once," she said softly. "The *kinner*—all of our *kinner*—struggling as they were, and your parents needing your help, and my *mamm* needing my help but not wanting it…"

"Maybe it was simpler than that," he replied. "I thought you were beautiful. You kind of liked me."

"You make me sound so cold," she laughed. "I more than 'kind of like' you, you silly man."

More? That felt like a victory, he had to admit. But then her smile slipped.

"I'm sorry if I made things weird between us when I cried," she went on. "I was treating you like you were more than just a friend, and that was wrong of me, and—"

Elias didn't want to hear any more of her recriminations—blaming herself for whatever this was that had sprung up between them. As if her vulnerability had been a problem! He'd been honored to be the man at her side, but he didn't quite know how to say that, so instead, he put his finger under her chin, tipped her surprised face up and then lowered his lips over hers.

Her words evaporated on her lips, and her eyes fluttered closed as he drew her in close against him. What he'd wanted was her in his arms, and now that she was here, he never wanted to let her go. She was warm and soft, and she felt like sunshine and comfort. The scent of moist earth and growing plants swirled around them, and when he finally, regretfully, pulled back from the kiss, he found Delia blinking up at him in such an endearingly bewildered way that he almost kissed her again.

"Don't apologize," he said. "We might have been putting up an act for our *kinner*, but what I've been feeling is real. And I don't want to hear you blame yourself for overstepping, or think you did anything that made me uncomfortable. You didn't."

"Oh…" she breathed. "What…what are you feeling?"

What was it? He felt protective of her and jealous at the thought of some other man courting her. He felt upside down and turned around, but in the best possible way. He trusted her; he wanted to know what she was thinking, and all he seemed to want lately was an excuse to be close to her again. Any excuse, really. He'd even return a borrowed box of garbage bags.

"What am I feeling?" he repeated slowly. "Delia, I know this is crazy and fast, and I don't expect you to feel anything back, but—" He shouldn't say it. He really shouldn't! He should stop now while he had any morsel of dignity left! "—I fell in love with you."

There. The words were out. But they were also true. While he and Delia had been pretending, he'd dropped all his defenses, and he'd fallen head over heels in love with Delia Swarey.

Delia's heart skipped a beat, and a fat bumblebee buzzed past them, bobbing through the warm, still air toward a flower. Outside, she could hear the boys calling to each other—something about the hose getting tangled. But she and Elias were tucked away in this greenhouse, his warm hands on her waist, and his chocolate brown eyes searching hers. Her face still felt tickled from where his beard had brushed against her when he'd kissed her.

She opened her mouth to say something, but nothing came out. Still, she couldn't tear her eyes away from his. She felt so protected and safe in his arms like this, and she desperately wanted it to last for as long as possible.

"I know it wasn't the plan," Elias said tenderly. "But I thought I sensed something more from you, too. Was I imagining it?"

"No, you didn't imagine it," she whispered. "When I said this had started to feel real, I meant that it wasn't pretend for me anymore. And I felt so foolish! Because we know what this was—it was playacting."

"It isn't for me anymore." His voice was deep and soft.

"Me, neither." She swallowed. "I'm in love with you, too."

Elias slid his arms tighter around her waist and touched his lips to hers. This time, she twined her arms around his neck and kissed him back just as ardently as he kissed her. His beard tickled her face, and his shoulders felt strong and reliable under her hands. This was nothing like courting as a young woman, shyly touching hands in the moonlight. This was entirely different— two grown adults who knew how courting worked, and marriage, too, for that matter, and her heart seemed to leap forward along with their life experience.

When she pulled back, Elias touched her chin with the pad of his thumb, and he looked tenderly down at her.

"I've been wanting to do that for a while," he murmured.

She took a step back, and he reluctantly released her.

Outside, she heard Moses's voice as he headed past, talking to Ezekiel. Her boys were trusting her to tell them the truth. And they weren't quite ready for a new step-*daet* yet. Maybe soon…but not like this. She couldn't damage their trust in her now.

"Are you okay?" Elias asked.

"Elias, we can't do this," she said quietly. "The *kinner* aren't ready. At least mine aren't. If you'd seen how they looked at me! *Yah*, I want to be able to move forward and get married again, but I need my boys in my life, too. If I rush this, I could lose them. This is pivotal. Moses is only eleven, and Thomas and Aaron might seem quite grown-up, but at fifteen and fourteen, they're still just overgrown boys. Their hearts are so tender and sensitive. Ezekiel might be able to handle it since he's almost old enough to marry, and I think Beulah might be the one—" She was rambling, and she knew it.

"They're not ready," he concluded.

"Is Violet?" she asked.

Elias licked his lips, then pressed them together in a thin line. "No, she's not. She was so relieved it wasn't real, and this morning she looked happier than I'd seen her in two years. She's not ready for this, either."

"You could lose her!" Delia said. "I know what it's like to be a thirteen-year-old girl. Everything feels bigger and more painful than it does to anyone else. Something you think is small is truly large for her! You don't want to push her away now."

Elias nodded. "You're right. I don't… But I also know that something like these feelings between us doesn't come along every day."

Delia's throat closed off with emotion. "I know…"

Because she'd known how special it was when she'd met Zeke. And she'd not felt that way again until she'd met Elias. But what about the *kinner*? They were the reason they'd come together to begin with, and they had to remain the priority.

"I wonder if they might get used to it," Elias said.

"Do you want to risk that?" Delia asked, and her lips quivered. "If Violet left the faith, I wouldn't forgive myself. If one of my boys left, or if my relationship with them suffered—" She could imagine how awful she'd feel if she'd put her own heart and companionship ahead of her children. "I know what it's like to be the child in a home who feels like they've been pushed aside."

"I wouldn't do that to your boys," he said earnestly.

"And I would never do that to Violet, either, but sometimes they feel it differently than we intend. My *mamm* married Joseph for herself, and I can see why! He loves her. He's standing by her. They are very much in love. But it was different for us *kinner* living through it. We went from being the center of our parents' world to our father being dead and our mother having another man to love. I'm not saying she was wrong, but it had far-reaching consequences."

Elias swallowed, then nodded slowly. "I don't want to pay that price, either."

"We've told our *kinner* that this isn't real…" she said. "I think we should stand by our word."

Even though it had become very real! But how could she go to her children now and tell them that she and Elias had changed their minds? The boys needed stability, security. Her boys needed her to choose them.

"Mamm?" she heard Thomas call. "Mamm, where are you?"

The screen door from the house slammed shut. The boys must have gone inside. She sucked in a breath.

"I should go," Elias said, his voice thick.

And Delia knew she must, but something tugged her back. She rose up onto her toes and kissed Elias on the cheek.

"If only things were different, Elias," Delia said, but emotion choked off her voice. Then she headed for the greenhouse door and didn't dare look back again.

This wasn't about her own heart. After *kinner* arrived, it never could be again. But she now knew exactly how much she'd be missing out on, and she wished so deeply that it could be different.

As she emerged into the sunlight, she saw Thomas standing on the step. He looked at her in surprise, and his gaze went over her shoulder. She glanced back. Elias came out of the greenhouse at the same time. She respected him for that—no hiding or sneaking.

"Yes, son?" Delia said.

"We, uh—" Thomas stopped.

"I'd best get the buggy to my parents' new place," Elias said. "See you later, Thomas. Glad to see you all working so hard to help your *mamm*."

But Delia could hear the sadness in his voice, too, even though he was trying to hide it.

"Anyway, we made peanut butter and jam sandwiches, Mamm," Thomas said. "Do you want one?"

"Actually, I'm not hungry right now, son," Delia said, and she forced a smile. "Why don't you boys eat, and I'll just finish up in the greenhouse."

"Okay, sure," Thomas said, then he paused. "Mamm, are you okay? You seem like you want to cry."

"I'm fine, son," she replied, blinking back a mist of tears that threatened to fall. "But thank you. Sometimes I just get emotional. That's all. I'll finish up in the greenhouse."

"Okay…" But Thomas didn't sound reassured at all.

And when Delia went back into the warm, humid greenhouse, she tugged the door solidly shut behind her and clamped a hand over her mouth. The tears started to flow, and she sank down onto the stool.

Delia loved that man. It was quick and crazy—he was right. But she'd already had one husband and buried him. She knew how this worked. There was no need to feel around and figure it out. She and Elias loved each other, and at their age, there were only two ways to go with those feelings. They either followed them and wed, or they broke things off and healed.

But healing from this heartbreak was going to be difficult—especially trying to hide it from her perceptive boys who'd follow their own testosterone-driven instincts and want to defend her.

So she took advantage of the brief time of solitude in the quiet, muffled air of the greenhouse, and she cried.

# Chapter Eleven

❦

"We told Violet we'd bring her along," Ezekiel said, dropping his straw hat onto his head. "If she's not next door anymore, what do we do?"

The day had been a long one for Delia, and her heart still felt heavy and clogged. She'd gotten through, though, mostly by focusing on the work in front of her, and she'd pushed herself past the point of exhaustion. She'd cleaned the greenhouse out, trimmed ornamental potted bushes, brushed down the horses and then started in on the kitchen. Everything smelled faintly of bleach now, and she still had a whole row of cupboards to empty and wash out…

Work was balm for the soul. Isn't that what she'd been taught all her life? And while it didn't heal a broken heart, it did help to distract her from her own pain while her *kinner* were watching.

"You could go by her grandparents' new place," Delia said. "You'd have to ask if it's all right if she went with you to the wiener roast. If Beulah's with you, her family shouldn't mind."

"Of course Beulah will be with us," Ezekiel said,

and a tender little smile touched his lips. "I always pick her up first."

"We told Violet that we'd bring her along," Thomas said. "So we'd better at least check."

Funny—the boys who had been so irritated with a girl helping out around the farm were now treating her like a friend. That was a good thing. Violet needed to see that there was plenty to stay Amish for—including good friends. And if Delia and Elias's little ploy had actually helped her to think a few things through, all the better.

"Did you want to come along, too, Mamm?" Moses asked.

"No, no," Delia said, running her fingers through his rumpled hair. "It's for the young people. You'll have fun."

"But you seem sad," Aaron said. "What are you going to do, clean cupboards?"

"Maybe," Delia said. "It's good to get it done. It smells nice in here, doesn't it? I feel better when things are clean. You boys go have fun, and I'll have a snack waiting for you when you get back."

"You'll be here?" Moses asked.

"Of course I'll be here. Where else would I be?"

With Elias—that was what they were all thinking. She'd told her boys it was all a ruse, but they didn't seem completely convinced. Things had changed between Delia and Elias, and Delia was doing her best to adjust to that. Elias hadn't been around for long, but she'd very quickly grown accustomed to his presence in her life. Too quickly. If she were giving her own boys advice, she'd tell them not to let their hearts go too easily—to wait, and be certain of the girl first. To not toy with something so precious as their own heartstrings. And yet, what had she done?

The boys headed out into the evening, and Delia sat down next to the window, watching the shadows grow longer as the sun sank in the west. She still had that row of cupboards to finish up, but somehow her drive to do it had evaporated now that she had her privacy. She'd cried a good deal the night before—but she'd been very careful to muffle any sound lest she worry the boys. The walls were thinner than she'd realized before, and the last thing she needed was for her overprotective brood to try to fix an adult-size problem with teenager solutions.

Somehow, she'd hoped that Elias would come by again, but he hadn't. *Of course* he hadn't. He knew where things stood as well as she did, and yet she did hope all the same.

"What is wrong with me?" Delia asked herself aloud, and she rose to her feet and headed back to the cupboards. She stepped up onto her step stool and started to empty the first top cupboard of its contents—large bowls and serving platters.

Delia was the one her friends came to for marriage advice. She was the one who was supposed to know how to handle relationships, and here she was with her heart in a knot as if she was a teenager herself. And she truly expected better from herself. She didn't dare go find some older, wiser woman to give her advice, because she was afraid of looking like a fool.

She sprayed the water and bleach mixture into the cupboard and followed it with a damp rag, wiping out dust in a brown smudge on her cloth.

*Gott, please help me to get over Elias*, she prayed. *I really didn't mean to fall in love with him.*

Outside, she heard the clop of hooves and the crunch of buggy wheels. Were the boys back? Did they forget something? Or was it Elias coming by to talk again?

Her heart gave a leap at the thought, and she backed down off her step stool and headed to the window. A buggy had stopped in front of the house, but it wasn't her *kinner* or Elias, either. It was Joseph. He climbed down from the driver's seat, and he had a basket over one arm, covered in a white cloth.

"Joseph?" she murmured.

Maybe her *mamm* needed her again. It looked like life was about to get busy again, and maybe that was an answer to prayer, too. Staying busy would keep her from brooding over Elias. Gott's blessings often arrived dressed like hard work. Wasn't that what people said?

She went to the door and opened it before Joseph even made it up the steps. She gave him what she hoped was a welcoming smile.

"Hello, Joseph," she said. "Come in. Would you like some coffee or tea?"

"*Danke*, I would," Joseph said. "Are you all right, Delia?"

"I'm—" She swallowed hard. "I think I will be."

Joseph gave her a thoughtful look as he passed her to come inside, and he took off his hat, revealing some disheveled hair and a bald spot. He looked down at his hat and then up at her again.

"Are you sure?" he asked.

"*Yah*. Of course. What can I do for you?"

"Well, I came to tell you about the doctor's appointment," he said. "Your *mamm* put up a bit of a fuss, but I reminded her that she'd promised you that she'd go, so she did. There were lots of tests done, and in the end, the doctor said that there's hope."

"There is?" Delia felt a genuine smile reach her face. "I'm so glad! What do you have to do?"

"It'll be some trial and error with different medications, but there are a couple of options that work well with patients like your *mamm*," he said. "And most times the medication helps an awful lot."

"That's wonderful news," Delia said, and she led the way inside. "I'm so glad, Joseph. I've been worried sick about her. Should I put on some tea? Or do you want decaf coffee?"

"Decaf would be nice," he replied, sitting down at the table.

Delia set about starting the coffee percolator, and when it was set on the stove to boil, she came back to the table.

"Delia, can I ask you something?" Joseph asked.

"Of course."

"What's really bothering you?" he asked. "And don't say it's nothing because I watched you grow up. And I know what you look like when you're truly upset, and that's what you look like right now."

"Do I?" she asked feebly.

"*Yah.* You do."

Joseph leaned his elbows on the table and met her gaze expectantly. She considered putting him off, but she doubted he'd accept it. And somehow, knowing she couldn't go to anyone else for advice made her stepfather suddenly seem like a better candidate.

"Can I trust your discretion, Joseph?" she asked.

"You have always been able to trust my discretion," he said. "I have never once told tales about the goings-on in our home. Never once."

"Well…"

And the story came out of her. How she and Elias had hoped to help their *kinner* through their issues surrounding their parents dating again and moving on, and how they'd leaned into each other and advised each other and supported each other and how the pretend relationship had suddenly gotten very real.

"But the *kinner* aren't ready for this, Joseph," she said. "That's why we started this facade to begin with! We wanted to help them start thinking about it."

"And what are the boys doing, exactly?" Joseph asked.

"Chasing off any man who shows interest! They're so afraid that I'll get hurt that they're trying to head off any man who might think I'd make a good wife. And the reality of the situation is, there aren't that many widowers to be had or single men my age. I do want to marry again, but I have to be careful…"

"Hmm." Joseph sucked in a deep breath. "And what is to say they won't settle into things once you choose someone?"

Did he remember a different home life?

"Joseph," she said gently, "when Mamm married you, it wasn't easy on us *kinner*. I know you were a kind and good man, but it was hard for us. What I needed was more time with my *mamm* to adjust to my *daet*'s death. I didn't get that."

"You understand why, though, don't you?" Joseph

asked. "The money was tight. She was tired and lonesome. She needed support, and…and I loved her dearly."

"*Yah*, I know. I understand even better now that I've lost Zeke," she said. "But Joseph, a new stepparent is a very difficult thing to navigate. Even for me, and I was Aaron's age when you and Mamm married. I had a lot of trouble adjusting to you. I'm sorry—that might be hard to hear."

"I know," he said, but his lined eyes looked sad all the same.

"It was very hard, Joseph. I know Mamm married you for herself. She loved you. You loved her. You were good for each other, but Mamm wasn't thinking about us *kinner*. At least I don't think she was. I don't want to put my *kinner* through that."

Joseph pursed his lips, then angled his head to the side in acceptance of her description.

"I didn't know how to be a *daet*," he said. "I thought I could learn. I really did! But I didn't know how to reach you. I didn't know how to show you that I was on your side. And you were already a teenager, and your *mamm* had you well in hand. I just let her continue, and I didn't get in the way."

"I really thought you didn't—" Delia felt tears in her eyes and she wiped an errant streak off her cheek. "I thought you didn't love us, Joseph."

"But I did!" Joseph leaned forward. "Does a man marry a woman with six *kinner*, work every day to bring home enough money to feed and clothe them all, and do it just for the wife? No! I loved you *kinner*, too. I just… I didn't know how to show it. I didn't know how to be a *daet* like the one you'd lost. I didn't think you needed me!"

"I didn't think I did, either," Delia said with a small smile. "But since when do *kinner* know about what they really need? I needed to be loved by my step*daet*."

"And you were, Delia." Joseph's chin quivered. "You were. I just didn't know how to be your new *daet*. And I don't think you knew how to love a new *daet*, either."

"Maybe not," she agreed. "I'm sorry, Joseph."

"Don't apologize for having been a confused young person," he said with a tender smile. "You did your best. Now, I've had many years to reflect on what I did right and what I did wrong, and I think I have some advice for you."

"Oh?" she said. "If you're going to tell me I should have protected my heart better, I know it already."

"No, not that," Joseph said with a frown. "But sometimes what a child needs is to learn how to love the new person in the family. You cannot bring Zeke back, Delia. Your loyalty to him is wasted. He's already gone. And you do need love and support in your home. You need a husband by your side. Perhaps what the boys need is not so much a home with only you and no father, but to learn how to love a good step*daet* who would be good to both you and them. Sometimes new *daets* and the *kinner* need to learn a few things together, and avoiding it doesn't help. I tried that path, and I regret it."

"Do you think so?" she asked slowly.

"I do," he said. "For what it's worth, of course. That's just my two cents' worth." He reached across the table and patted her hand. "And you are much like your mother. She always had to get her reassurance from Gott.

So that's my take, but pray on it, Delia. See if maybe there's wisdom in there somewhere. If not, throw it out."

"Oh, Joseph," she said with a teary smile. "Thank you. I will give it some thought and prayer."

How much had she missed out on through the years by avoiding a relationship with her stepfather? How much advice had he held back? How much support could she have gotten from a loving stepfather? He wasn't her real *daet*—that was true. But he'd been there, and she'd missed out.

How much would her own boys miss out on if they stayed on this path of overprotecting her and pushing away a stepfather who might love them dearly?

She did need to pray on this…because it sounded to her like Joseph was talking sense. And maybe there was hope for a future with Elias, after all. Maybe!

"You just seem to be in a bad mood, Elias," his mother said frankly.

Elias sat in the big, airy kitchen of the main house, where his sister Dina and their mother puttered about setting an arrangement of date squares and shoofly pie onto the table. His parents' little *dawdie hus* that was on this property was now full of boxes and bags, and it would be a few days, or even weeks, before it was arranged properly so that Mamm could take over the cooking again in their own little house. Until then, they'd be eating their meals and spending their evenings with Dina and her family.

"I'm not in a bad mood. I'm worried about my daughter's lateness," Elias replied. "She should have been home half an hour ago."

"And you never stayed out a minute past your curfew?" Dina teased. "I remember how you used to be the last teen to leave! The hosts would be blinking and yawning, and you'd still be chatting away!"

"I might have, but this is different."

"Not so much," Dina replied. "Be calm. She'll be back. I've said it before, but having only one child means that you focus on her too much. Would you be panicking if you had three younger ones using up your attention? Not likely."

His sister meant well, and she was probably right, but it wasn't helping right now.

"Dina, she's late. And she's a girl, not a teenage boy like I was."

"She'd only be late if she had left right away, and the hymn singing didn't go long. She's probably making friends," his father said. "I remember how late you could be, too. And you were never in trouble. You were enjoying yourself with good people. That was all. She's with good people, Elias."

Elias didn't answer, because they were all probably right. She was in good company, and she'd show up pretty soon, no doubt, but something in his gut wouldn't give him peace.

Elias's oldest niece, ten-year-old Fannie, appeared at the top of the stairs in her white nightgown, bare toes poking out from underneath and her hair pulled back in a blond braid. She looked a lot like Violet had not too long ago. The years had passed by awfully quickly.

"Fannie, you should be in bed," Dina said.

"But you have treats," Fannie begged.

"These are for grown-ups, and you can have some in the morning," Dina said. "Off to bed with you."

Dina's husband, Bart, got up to go tuck his daughter back into bed, and Elias couldn't help but smile as Bart swiped a date square off the plate on his way by. Fannie would have a little treat, after all. *Daets* had soft places in their hearts for their little girls.

"All right, then," Elias's father said, meeting Elias's gaze. "I can see that you're worried. If you want to drive out to the farm, I could show you the way."

That was a good idea. Something about this didn't sit right with him.

"The Swarey farm is closer," his mother interjected. "They are what…a fifteen-minute drive away? And they're on the way to the Beiler farm, anyway. Why not nip over there and see if her boys are back? Then you know if you need to worry. Those are good *kinner*, Elias. Very good. If she's with the four of them, she's safe, I promise you that."

A better idea, actually. But after telling Delia how he felt, it was going to be awkward to go over there unannounced. Maybe she wouldn't want to see him… All the same, his daughter's safety trumped all of that.

"I'll head over to Delia's place," Elias said. "And if her boys are home, one of them can guide me back to the Beiler farm."

His father helped him to hitch up the buggy, and Elias pointedly ignored his sister and mother in the window as he turned on the battery-operated headlights, flicked the reins, and the horse pulled the buggy up the drive. They thought he was being overprotective—they didn't hide that fact.

But was he overreacting? He certainly hoped not. If Violet arrived back at the farm while he was off looking for her, it would be a whole lot of worry for nothing on his part. But somehow he felt better doing something other than sitting around waiting.

Besides, all day he'd been around people—his parents, his sister, the *kinner*…and he hadn't had any time alone to just let his thoughts and feelings settle. Somehow, Delia was still front and center in his mind, and he couldn't push thoughts of her away. The truth was he missed her. Desperately.

What was wrong with him that he couldn't simply set thoughts of her aside? Wasn't this part of what they wanted to show the young people—how to date someone chastely, without any regrets, and to be able to respect boundaries and move on? What kind of example was he turning out to be? Not a good one! He hadn't dated or courted in twenty years, and apparently, he was no better at this than an inexperienced young man! And he *should* be.

So yes, he was wound-up and worried about his daughter, but he'd been wound-up all day. Was he reacting like this to Violet's lateness because of his own heartbreak? He hoped not. He couldn't be the kind of father who took out his own emotional issues on his daughter. That was an excellent way to push her away!

As the horse trotted down the road, hooves clopping merrily, Elias attempted to sort out his feelings. He'd fallen in love with Delia, and that was his problem— no one else's.

*Gott, please help me to let go of her*, he prayed earnestly. *Loving her is only hurting myself. I know that. I can see it. Help me to let her go.*

When he arrived at Delia's farm, the lights in the house were glowing warmly from the downstairs windows. Upstairs was dark, but the kitchen and sitting room were both alight, and he felt a rush of warmth.

Delia took a house and made it a home. Her boys didn't know how blessed they were with a mother like her. As if on cue, Delia appeared in the window, and his heart stuttered in his chest. She had that effect on him, it seemed. Would it be easier once he and Violet went home again, and he wouldn't have any more reason to see her again? Maybe that was the secret—physically leaving—although the thought was a sad one.

Elias scanned the area in the swath of light from his headlamps, but he didn't see Ezekiel's buggy. He tied off his reins and hopped down to the ground. Delia opened the side door and shaded her eyes. She was outlined by a golden glow from the kerosene lights inside.

"Elias?" She sounded a little breathless.

"Hi," he said. "Is it okay that I came by?"

*"Yah, yah,* of course." A smile spread over her face, and he could tell that she'd missed him as much as he'd missed her. Her brown eyes shone with warmth, and he couldn't help remembering that the last time he'd looked into them, he'd been holding her in his arms. He was only making this harder on them, wasn't he?

"I'm sorry to just stop in like this," he said. "But my daughter isn't back yet, and I wanted to see if your boys had made it home."

"No, not yet," she replied.

"Oh…" So maybe he was overreacting a bit. "My

family thought I was overreacting. I might be. Is this later than usual?"

Her smile softened.

"It is, I'll admit," she said. "It's okay to worry, you know."

"Tell my sister that. She's been teasing me something fierce." He smiled ruefully.

"Why don't you come inside?" Delia asked. "I'm sure the boys will be back any minute, and when they are, you'll know that they dropped Violet off safe and sound."

"Do you mind?" he asked.

"Of course not," she said. "It's actually very nice to see you. I'd wondered if you'd come by again." Her voice caught.

"I wanted to, but I thought—" He headed up the steps, and he paused when he reached her. She was soft, and smelled faintly of soil. She must have been out working with the plants until late, and he found that little detail endearing. "I thought you'd want me to stay away."

"I'm glad you didn't," she said softly.

He wanted to kiss her again, and it took all of his self-control not to. Besides, he was here for Violet, and if that fact didn't sober him, nothing would. There was no future with Delia, no matter how much he wanted one.

The clop of hooves sounded at the top of the drive, and Elias turned to see the bobbing headlamps of Ezekiel's buggy coming down the drive.

"There they are," Delia said.

"I feel a little foolish," he admitted, casting her a rueful smile, but he also felt a rush of relief. They'd be home, and his worry would be for nothing.

Delia nodded. "I do understand. You're a good father, you know."

The compliment was sweet coming from her, and somehow it landed a little deeper, too. He hoped he was a good enough father to keep his daughter both safe and on the right side of the fence. And at the same time, he found himself wishing he'd gotten just a few more moments alone with Delia. They'd be stolen moments, and they wouldn't contribute to any kind of future together, but they'd have been a balm to his aching heart all the same.

Maybe it was better not to have that time with her. It wouldn't make letting her go any easier, would it?

Ezekiel pulled his buggy up next to Elias's, and Elias tried to school his features so that he looked calmer than he felt. He was feeling downright ridiculous now, having come out here in a fluster, worried about his daughter who had probably arrived home just as he left.

"Evening, Elias," Ezekiel said, hopping down.

"Good evening," Elias said. "Did you have a good time?"

"*Yah*, it was good—" Ezekiel glanced back at his brothers, then winced. "I'm sorry I didn't bring Violet back. I understand that it was my responsibility to bring her, but—"

Elias's heart thundered in his own ears.

"You didn't bring her back?" Elias cut in, his voice harsher than he intended.

"She wouldn't come back with us," Moses piped up, hopping down from the back of the buggy. "And we tried!"

"What do you mean, she wouldn't come back?" he

demanded, and his voice must have been more intimidating than he'd intended, because Moses took a step back and Ezekiel squared his shoulders. He felt a gentle hand on his arm, and he looked down to find Delia at his side.

"Let them explain," she said.

"Sorry." He swallowed. "What happened? Where is she?"

"She went off with Liam—the Englisher boy," Ezekiel said. "I didn't see her go, but Aaron and Thomas did."

"I didn't see her go, either," Moses piped in.

"Where did they go?" Elias turned to Aaron and Thomas.

"In Liam Speicher's car," Thomas said. "They were going off for a drive together. I told them that you wouldn't like it."

"In his car?" Elias erupted.

"*Yah*, he came in a red car. And everyone was looking at it."

"And what did they say when you said I wouldn't like it?" Elias demanded.

"Violet said you wouldn't mind," Thomas said, and his ears turned red. "And Liam said they wouldn't be long, but they didn't come back, and everyone else was leaving, so we came home. We didn't want our *mamm* to worry."

Violet said he wouldn't mind! That was some impudence there!

"I'm sorry," Ezekiel said. "I take full responsibility for it. It's not my brothers' fault. I probably should have kept a better eye on where she was."

"It's not your fault, Ezekiel—she's old enough to make better choices than that," Elias said. "So she's off in a car with some Englisher boy? Where would they have gone?"

"I have an idea, actually," Ezekiel said. "There's a spot by a stream where young people like to park and… talk…"

Right. The very stream he'd stopped at to comfort Delia. He knew it well, and he rubbed his hands over his face.

"That would be my best guess," Ezekiel said. "If not there, they could have gone into town for fast food or something…"

"I'll go see if I can find her," Elias said. "*Danke* for telling me what you know."

"Actually—" Delia's voice was firm, but quiet. "I don't think you should do that."

Elias turned around and shot Delia a look of surprise. "You do know what Englisher boys want to do in their cars, don't you?"

Something quite close to what he and Delia had been doing in the same spot—although he and Delia had been much more chaste and well-meaning than that boy would be.

"I do," she said with a nod. "But I think you should let my boys go out there to find her. If you go out there, find her and march her back, she'll be angry at you for years. Fairly? No. But angry. However, if you let the boys go and fetch her home, it gives her a chance to make the right choice on her own. If she chooses the right thing, then you're miles ahead with her. I promise you that."

"And you don't mind your boys doing this for me?" he asked.

"Are you willing, boys?" Delia asked, turning her attention over his shoulder.

"*Yah*, I'll go," Ezekiel said. "I should have brought her home, and I'll make this right."

He was a responsible young man, and Elias was grateful for him.

"We'll go, too," Thomas said. "It's only right."

"And I'm going!" Moses added. "If they're all going, I want to, too!"

"Fine, fine, but stay together and bring Violet straight back," Delia said. "And if she won't come, then Elias will go, and I'll go find Liam's grandparents. Liam has to go back home sometime, and I know Art Speicher won't be allowing that kind of behavior to continue."

And somehow Delia's no-nonsense plan soothed his frustration better than anything else could. She was thinking ahead about things he wasn't even considering yet in his shocked state. Her head was more level than his was right now, and he was grateful for her in this moment.

"Do you think this will work?" Elias asked.

"I think so," Delia replied, and she put that reassuring hand on his arm again. "Give her the chance to do the right thing, Elias. I think she has it in her."

## Chapter Twelve

Delia set a cup of tea in front of Elias and nudged a plate of bread closer to him. He recognized this loaf as one his mother had sent over the other day, and he picked some up. They'd been waiting now for nearly half an hour, and Delia was mentally calculating how long it would take her boys to get to the creek and back again.

From the wall next to the calendar, the clock ticked softly, but oh, so slowly. She could only imagine his worry right now, and all she could do was try to comfort him with what she had on hand—his mother's baking and a cup of tea.

"We had just talked about this, Delia," Elias said, shaking his head. "We'd just talked about what it would mean if she jumped the fence. How she'd be leaving her family behind, and how I couldn't be there for her the way she'd need. I really thought I'd gotten through to her!"

Delia sat down in the seat kitty-corner to his, and she felt some heat in her own face. "I think we both know that understanding there is no future with someone doesn't take away the feelings…"

Elias paused, then smiled ruefully. "*Yah*, but that's no comfort right now, Delia."

"My point is, tonight doesn't mean she's making any permanent decisions. She's just…reacting. Not thinking. Like teenagers do."

Elias sighed. "Would you be this calm if this were one of your *kinner*?"

If this were Ezekiel or Thomas or Aaron? She'd be hopping mad, and she'd be looking to Elias for some sort of perspective on how teenage boys thought.

"No," she said. "If this were reversed, you'd be calming me down. I'd be a wreck."

"Somehow, that makes me feel better," he said, and he cast her a tender smile.

"I was going to tell you that my stepfather came by today," she said.

"Joseph? Is your *mamm* okay?" he asked.

"*Yah.* There is medication that will help her," she said. "Thank Gott!"

"That's good news," he said.

"But more than that," she went on. "I had a good talk with Joseph about what it was like after he married my *mamm*. I felt ignored, but so did he."

"He really opened up?" Elias asked.

"He did." She felt her eyes mist with the memory. "He didn't know how to be a step*daet*, and I realized that I didn't know how to accept another father into my life. He meant well, though. Joseph is a good man."

"I always thought he was, too," Elias said. "Does that mean you and he have…made peace?"

"I think we have," Delia said. "He pointed out that sometimes what we need most is to learn how to accept someone into our lives—not to avoid it. And he had wanted to be more in our lives, but he hadn't known how."

"That's insightful," he murmured.

"He also said that *kinner* don't know what they need. They just…need! And sometimes what they need is to have a stepparent know how to love them, and accept them. I know that for me, I lost out on a lot of love and support that could have been mine if I'd only known how to accept a new *daet* in our home."

Elias stilled, and for three ticks of that clock, he didn't move. Did he understand yet what she'd realized? She wasn't sure how to bring this up—not gracefully, at least. His gaze moved up to meet hers, questions shining in his eyes.

"Do you mean—" he started, but then the sound of hooves and wheels cut him off. She sighed. There was no more time. Maybe Gott was intervening, and she shouldn't tell him what she'd realized. There were *kinner* who needed their parents right now. Just because they loved each other didn't mean they belonged together, either.

Elias stood up and went over to the window, shading his eyes. For a moment he stood there with the tension of a coiled spring, and then his shoulders relaxed.

"There she is…" he said.

His daughter. That was where his heart belonged. Delia joined him at the window. Ezekiel had already gotten out of the buggy, and Violet was climbing down with a hand from Ezekiel. Her face was tearstained, and the other boys hopped down after her. There was the sound of boys' chatter, and Violet wiped her face with the flat of her hand.

Delia put a hand on Elias's shoulder, and he looked down at her.

"Okay... Okay..." He swallowed hard. "I can't mess this up."

Delia knew what he was worried about—saying the wrong thing, showing anger or maybe not showing enough! She knew he was worried about getting this wrong and having it affect Violet for the rest of her life, but from where Delia stood, what Violet needed was her *daet*'s love. That was it.

"Just go hug her," Delia said.

He nodded and headed for the side door, but before he could get there, it was flung open and Moses came in, followed by Aaron. The other boys would be unhitching the buggy, Delia imagined. Violet came up behind, and when she appeared in the doorway of the mudroom, her face crumpled, and instead of going to her father, she dashed past him and flung herself into Delia's arms.

Delia instinctively wrapped her arms around the girl, and she shot Elias a look of wide-eyed surprise. He just shrugged, and Delia patted the girl's back.

"I think this calls for a girl talk," Delia said quietly. "It's okay."

"I feel...so...so...stupid!" Violet sobbed.

"Stupid? Never," Delia said, and pulled back, looking into Violet's blotchy, teary face. "Do you hear me? You are not stupid. You are now wiser. There is a difference."

The boys stared at her in uncomfortable silence, and Delia turned her attention back to Violet.

"What happened?" she asked gently.

"He said he'd take me for a drive," she hiccuped. "And then he stopped by the creek, and I knew why he'd done it then. I'd wanted to get a burger, but he said this was better. And I said I only wanted to talk, and he said that was okay, but I didn't like being out there in the dark alone, and I knew I'd messed up then—"

A sound close to a growl came out of Elias's throat, and Delia cast him an annoyed look. Now was not the time!

"And then?" she asked softly.

"Then we talked, and he told me about his school and all that, and it didn't sound as free and fun as I thought it would be, and it sounded kind of scary, actually. And he had cigarettes and he wanted me to try one, and I didn't like the smell…"

The story tumbled out of her—a tale as old as time. A more experienced boy and a naive girl. Liam hadn't crossed any lines, but he'd tried to impress her with his Englisher life and his bad habits. He'd tried to look mature and tough, and all he'd succeeded in doing was scaring the poor girl.

"And then Ezekiel and Aaron and Thomas and Moses showed up," she said, her voice wavering. "And they said my *daet* was so mad, and I'd better get into the buggy so I could go home."

"What did Liam do?" Delia asked.

"He said I could stay with him if I wanted," she said. "And I said I'd better go home, so he said okay. But I was so glad to see them come to fetch me! I've never been so glad to see a pack of stupid boys in my life!"

"Stupid boys?" Moses said. "We're not stupid! We rescued you!"

Violet cast the boy an apologetic look. "*Yah*, you did. Thanks, Moses."

Moses straightened his shoulders, and if he could have grown two inches right there, he would have. Ezekiel and Thomas came inside then, kicking off their boots and tossing their hats onto the pegs on the wall.

"You know, I didn't like the idea of having four brothers when I thought our parents were courting," Violet said, "but I can see how you all would come in handy."

The boys rolled their eyes, but Delia could tell that Violet's comment had pleased them.

"We always kinda wanted a sister," Aaron said in a soft voice.

And Delia had always wanted a daughter to add to her family, but Gott hadn't given her that little girl she'd longed for. Sometimes they had to trust Gott to know better.

"So long as that sister didn't get us into all kind of trouble," Thomas added with a laugh.

Delia gave Violet a squeeze. The boys were only teasing, and she didn't want Violet's feelings to get hurt.

"Sweetie, I think you learned something tonight," Delia said. "You aren't quite as grown-up as you thought, are you?"

"I don't think I am," Violet said, and her lips trembled.

"That Liam kid is some piece of work," Thomas said as he came into the kitchen. "Someone's got to talk to his grandparents. Taking off with a girl three years younger! Who does that? He scared her pretty badly, too!"

"I'll talk to them," Ezekiel muttered.

"You will not!" Delia said, raising her voice. "There are two adults in this room, and Violet's father to boot! If Elias doesn't have the time to talk to them and wants me to, then I will do it. But you are *kinner* in this home, and you will remember that. It is up to Elias to deal with things as he sees fit!"

Ezekiel cast his mother a rueful look, but she refused to back down. Her boys were not going to try to fix this one.

"Violet," Delia whispered. "I knew you'd make the right choice."

*"Yah?"* Violet wiped her eyes. "What made you so sure?"

"You have a good heart," she replied. "I saw it before, and I see it now. I know this was a scary night, and a lot happened, but I want you to remember that you made the right choice. Okay? And you came back."

Violet nodded. *"Danke,* Delia."

Delia looked over at Elias, who stood to the side, his arms crossed over his broad chest. He looked filled to the brim with emotion with nowhere to vent it.

"Right now, your *daet* needs one thing from you," Delia said.

"What?" Violet looked over at him, and Delia could see the nervousness in the girl. She knew she'd caused trouble, and she'd get a lengthy lecture later on.

"He needs a hug," Delia said.

Violet walked over to where her father stood and she looked up at him, her arms limp at her sides.

"I'm sorry, Daet—" she whispered, and her chin trembled.

Elias reached out, wrapped his arms around his daughter and crushed her against his chest. Tears shone in his eyes. No, Violet was not half so grown-up as she'd thought. Delia was just glad she was back safely.

Elias released his daughter, and Violet heaved a sigh. Her tears seemed to be spent now, and she and Delia exchanged a tender look. How would he have dealt with this alone? If it weren't for Delia, he would have driven out there himself, demanded his daughter get into his buggy, and he'd have torn a strip off that Liam kid that he'd never forget. He would have reacted in anger, and he would likely have affected his relationship with his daughter for the rest of his life.

But he hadn't. Thanks to Delia...

What was it that she'd said about her step*daet*, that he'd needed to learn how to be a father in their home, and the *kinner* needed to learn to love him, too? Something like that... Was there any chance she felt the same way about her own home?

Delia had her back turned now, and she was rummaging around in a cupboard, pulling down some snacks for the *kinner*. It wasn't a bad idea—they'd all be hungry after that excitement, and Violet moved off to talk to Aaron and Thomas, where Thomas was loudly stating his unfavorable opinion about Liam Speicher.

Ezekiel came to where Elias stood, and the teenager scrubbed a hand through his unruly hair. "Elias, I just wanted to say that I'm sorry I let you down earlier. I should have gone after your daughter right away, and—"

"Ezekiel, you're a fine young man," Elias said, interrupting him. "You made the best choice you could in the moment, and you put your *mamm*'s worry first. That was a good choice. I'm glad you take good care of her. Man to man? I respect that."

Ezekiel looked startled, then he nodded. "*Danke*, Elias. I do try to help Mamm out as best I can. She doesn't like me to do it, but someone has to."

Someone, indeed, but there was no one Elias wanted

to be taking care of Delia except himself. He wanted the job more than anything…if she could see a way forward with him.

"What if there was another man who wanted to help in that mission to make your *mamm* happy?" Elias asked.

"You?" Ezekiel guessed.

*"Yah…"* His heartbeat sped up, and suddenly the opinion of this seventeen-year-old kid mattered to him a great deal.

"What about me and my brothers?"

"Well, I know there's no replacing your *daet*, but I'd like to be a different kind of *daet*. I'd want to help you, and give you advice if you'd take it and support your *mamm* in what she wants you four to do. I always wanted some boys of my own, and I'd be honored more than you can imagine if you'd let me treat you like my own."

"Then I guess you'd have to convince Mamm," Ezekiel said with a small smile. "And Moses will probably give you some grief over it, but if Mamm agrees, I could talk him into it."

"And Thomas and Aaron?" Elias asked.

"They'll be okay if I'm okay."

That was exactly what Elias had thought. "Then maybe I'll have a word with your *mamm*."

"Mamm?" Ezekiel said, raising his voice. He headed over to where his mother was setting out plates, and there was a muted exchange. Ezekiel took the plates, and Delia came over to where Elias stood.

"Elias?" she said. "Please stay to eat. You aren't leaving now, are you? I'd hoped, I mean…" She swallowed.

"Can we talk alone?" he asked in a quiet voice. "Outside, maybe?"

She nodded and looked over her shoulder. The boys weren't even looking in their direction, and Violet was in an animated conversation with Aaron. Ezekiel gave them a sidelong look, and then pointedly ignored them.

"Sure," Delia said.

They slipped out the side door, and Elias caught her hand and led her away from the house a little ways. Then he slid his hand around her waist, drew her in close and kissed her. Her eyes fluttered shut, and she exhaled a sigh. When he pulled back, she looked anxiously toward the house again.

"I love you," Elias said.

"I know! I love you, too, but the *kinner*—"

"Don't always know what they need," he said. "You said that before, didn't you? Delia, my daughter doesn't think she's ready for this, but if it weren't for you, I would have mishandled everything tonight. Violet needs you. She does! I need you, too. And I talked to Ezekiel, and he figures he could get his brothers on board with this if I could only convince you."

"Really?" Delia stared up at him. "You won over Ezekiel?"

"Sure did." He shot her an exultant smile. "But I only did it with honesty. Delia, if you'd marry me, I'll treat your boys like my own. I'll love them and guide them and sacrifice anything I have to in order to give them the life they deserve. If you could love Violet the same way…"

Tears welled in Delia's eyes, and she nodded. "I already do!"

"Marry me," Elias pleaded. "Let's make this real. Let's plan a wedding, and make all of us one big family.

It won't always be easy, but I'll promise to make all six of you my very top priority on this green earth. What do you say?"

The side door opened then, and Moses appeared in the doorway.

"What's going on, Mamm?" Moses called.

"Get back inside," Ezekiel said from behind him.

"No! Something's wrong," Moses said.

"Nothing's wrong, Moses," Delia said.

"Then what's happening?" the boy demanded.

"I'm asking your mother to marry me," Elias said, raising his voice.

There was silence, then the faces of the other *kinner* appeared in the doorway, backlit with that soft glow of kerosene light. Maybe it was only fitting that all of them were here together, because if she said yes—and he prayed that she would—they'd be a package deal, all seven of them!

"What did she say?" Violet asked.

Elias turned back to Delia, and he looked down at her, his heart hovering in his chest.

"*Yah*, what do you say?" he whispered.

Delia nodded. "*Yah*. I will marry you, Elias!"

He dipped his head down and caught her lips with his. All he cared about was sealing this agreement with a kiss, and the *kinner* behind them started to chatter.

"What did she say?" That was Moses.

"She said yes, you doofus! That's why she's kissing him!" Aaron retorted. Or maybe that had been Thomas.

"Are we going to be siblings, then?" That was Violet. "Are you all going to be my stupid brothers?"

Then the *kinner* were laughing, and Violet squealed—

probably poked by one of the boys—and Elias's heart was so full he felt like he could burst. He couldn't wait to marry her. He couldn't wait to be the new *daet* to all four of her wonderful boys and for Violet to get the chance at having a *mamm* as lovely and thoughtful and wise as Delia.

Elias couldn't wait to make Delia his.

# Epilogue

Delia and Elias got married in mid-September when the flowers in the field were all harvested—or drooping as the nights got cooler and the leaves started to change color. It was a quick wedding, and before they said their vows, Elias had gone back to Indiana for a few weeks to take care of things there. He told his family about his upcoming nuptials, and gave his job his two-weeks' notice… Because Elias was going to be helping Delia and the boys run their flower farm.

The boys had worked hard, but with school, they needed to focus on learning and stop worrying about adult responsibilities.

The wedding was held at the Knussli farm. Adel, the community matchmaker, insisted. She'd been searching for a match for Delia, and she said it was the least she could do to support Delia in finding a husband the old-fashioned way.

So when the day of the wedding arrived, Delia found herself alone in the laundry room, standing next to the wringer washer and fiddling with the hem of her apron, her heart in her throat. The door creaked open, and Adel poked her head inside.

Adel was largely pregnant now with her second baby. Her little boy was now walking, and he was probably outside with the older girls having fun.

"Are you all right, Delia?" Adel asked.

*"Yah,"* Delia replied. "I'm just remembering my first wedding."

"Ah." Adel came inside and shut the door behind her. "I understand that very well. You and I both lost our first husbands."

"That's right—you understand," Delia said.

"What is worrying you most?" Adel asked.

"That it won't be the same," Delia said, her voice shaking.

"It won't be," Adel replied, running a hand over her rounded belly. "It will be completely different. This is a different man. There will be different challenges and different joys. It will be nothing like being married to Zeke. It will be everything like being married to Elias."

"Am I selfish to be doing this?" Delia asked. "Tell me the truth. I love Elias so much! And I think he'll be a wonderful stepfather for my sons, but—"

"Come." Adel went to the door, opened it and looked both ways. "The way is clear. Come on!"

Delia looked at Adel in surprise. The woman didn't sneak very well at this stage of her pregnancy, but Delia followed her all the same to an office. Adel ushered Delia inside and then brought her to a window.

"Look," Adel said.

Outside the window, she saw her boys lined up in front of Elias. Elias tugged at Aaron's collar, then tugged at a wrinkle on Ezekiel's sleeve. He said something she couldn't hear, and all four boys laughed. Violet joined them, and they turned away, moving out of sight again.

"Are you selfish for marrying him?" Adel asked. "You tell me."

"He's a wonderful father," Delia said softly.

"And you are a wonderful mother for choosing him," Adel said. "I promise you that."

They would be fine, wouldn't they? Elias would love her boys and give them the manly direction they needed. And Delia would love Violet with all her heart and relish having a daughter in her home. If love alone could keep that girl Amish, then Elias would never have to worry again, because Delia had love enough for all of them.

"Are you ready to go get married?" Adel asked.

"*Yah*, I am!" Delia said, and she pulled Adel into a hug. "Thank you!"

"I wish I could take the credit for this wedding, but Gott was the matchmaker with you two!" Adel laughed.

And Adel was right. Somehow, two lonely parents had found just what their families needed in each other. Gott put the lonely in families—that's what the Good Book said. And Delia's heart was overflowing.

She couldn't wait to start her life as Elias's wife and the loving, doting, proud *mamm* of five!

\* \* \* \* \*

*If you liked this story from Patricia Johns,
check out her previous Love Inspired books:*

An Amish Mother for His Child
Their Amish Marriage Arrangement
Their Amish Secret
Their Amish Matchmaking Dilemma

*Available now from Love Inspired!
Find more great reads at
www.LoveInspired.com.*

Dear Reader,

My son is a teenager, and we're now in the thick of parenting an almost-adult. We're teaching him to drive, giving him space to make his own choices and encouraging him to be all that he can be. It's exciting!

Is it a romantic time in our marriage, though? You might think that the parents of teens have no romance left in their lives, but I beg to differ. My husband and I might be getting older, but we still adore each other, and there is nothing more romantic than knowing we're in this together. That's the kind of love that I wanted to show in this story.

If you enjoyed this book, please consider leaving a review. Reviews really help an author to get the word out about her books, and that in turn helps to keep me writing.

I hope you'll check out some of my other stories. They're all listed on my website at patriciajohns.com. Take a look—you might find your next read! If you'd like to connect, I have a newsletter where I hold monthly giveaways, and I'd love it if you signed up. As always, if you'd like to reach out and say hello, don't be shy! It's always an honor to hear from my readers.

*Patricia*

## HARLEQUIN
### Reader Service

# Enjoyed your book?

Try the perfect subscription for Romance readers and get more great books like this delivered right to your door.

See why over 10+ million readers have tried Harlequin Reader Service.

**Start with a Free Welcome Collection with free books and a gift—valued over $20.**

Choose any series in print or ebook. See website for details and order today:

## TryReaderService.com/subscriptions

RSBPA24R